The
BROWNIE
ANNUAL
1975

Published by special arrangement with
THE GIRL GUIDES ASSOCIATION

Illustrated by PHIL GASCOINE

PURNELL

ONE DAY IN JORDAN

by Nora Blaze

"I can't understand it, Mariam*," said Leila. "We've stood here for over an hour and not a single car has stopped to buy our flowers."

The two girls in their Jordanian Brownie uniforms, dark-brown, with light-brown tie, socks and badge, stood beside the busy highway that leads from Jerusalem to the coast. They had been clambering about all morning on the steep, rocky hillside, picking great bunches of the cyclamen and anemones that grew wild in profusion. The hot spring sunshine of the Holy Land spread its golden light over the countryside, and larks sang joyfully in the deep-blue sky.

"With all these tourists from Jerusalem," sighed Leila again, "you'd think one of them would like some flowers, wouldn't you?"

"Yes," Mariam agreed, "and we did expect to make a nice lot of money for the Brownie funds. Here comes another!" She held out a glowing bunch of anemones, smiling her Brownie smile; but the car, full of people, swept past, leaving a cloud of dust hanging in the air.

The girls watched it disappear. Then Mariam picked up her basket full of flowers, and said, "It's no good. We shall just have to take them home to our mothers. Come on, Leila, the Jerusalem bus will be here soon. We must go back down the road to the stop."

They walked along with their baskets, keeping carefully against the foot of the hillside, for there was no pavement out here in the country and the road was busy with all kinds of traffic. They rounded a bend, and then Leila cried, "Oh!"

"What is it?" asked Mariam, following close behind.

They picked great bunches of flowers

*Arabic for Mary.

IT'S ALL HERE

SBN 361 02843 1
Copyright © 1974 PURNELL BOOKS,
Berkshire House, Queen Street, Maidenhead, Berks.
Made and printed in Great Britain by
Purnell & Sons Ltd., Paulton (Somerset) and London

Cover pictures show Brownies of the Bosmere and Bramford District having fun out of doors and watching sausages being sizzled for them, and, at side, Karen Edwards of the 5th Farnham (Bourne) Pack

"Well! No wonder no one wanted our flowers. Just look at that!"

Mariam looked ahead to where she was pointing. A small Arab peasant girl stood at the roadside, just as they had been doing, holding out bunches of flowers. But cars were stopping for her, and money was being given to her by smiling people in return for her cyclamen and anemones. Her flat round basket was nearly empty.

The Brownies rushed up to her.

"It's too bad!" Leila cried indignantly. "We need money for our Brownie funds and you are stopping all the cars! We can't sell our flowers with you here!"

The girl's dark eyes gazed up at her in bewilderment. She was very poorly dressed in the long black gown of a Bedouin girl. The gown was ragged and torn. There was a thin white head-veil over the girl's dark plaits. Her feet were bare on the hot, dusty road.

"I do not understand," she stammered. "All morning I have picked the flowers. I sell them to the rich ladies in the cars."

"Yes, we can see that," Leila said impatiently. "We want to sell ours, too! Let's stand here and sell them," she

suggested to Mariam. "It seems to be a good place."

They set down their baskets, and, lifting some bunches, held them out to the next car that came along. It stopped at once. The American ladies in it bought several bunches and paid for them, and the car shot off again.

"There, I told you!" Leila said triumphantly. "It's easy. We'll soon sell all our flowers and make a heap of money!"

The Bedouin girl burst into tears.

"You will take all my customers," she sobbed bitterly. "Why do you want to

"I do not understand," said the Arab girl

7

sell flowers? You have fine clothes; you don't need money!"

"Fine clothes!" Leila laughed. "These are our Brownie uniforms!"

The child continued to sob.

"You don't know what Brownies are?" Mariam asked gently.

The girl shook her head dumbly.

"We help other people," Mariam began to explain.

"I, too!" cried the child, stifling her sobs. "I, too, help! My mother and father are very poor, so I come each day to sell the flowers. My mother is very happy when I give her this money."

"What is your name?" asked Mariam kindly.

"I am called Aziza."

"Aziza," repeated Mariam thoughtfully. "It means 'dear one', doesn't it? Well, you *are* a dear to help your mother like this. Where do you live?"

Aziza pointed to where an Arab village of flat-roofed stone huts sprawled over the barren hillside.

"You come?" she invited. "I show you my house?"

They followed her up a steep track and came to the village, where Aziza led them to her home. It was just one big room, with no furniture. There were goat-skin mats on the earth floor, mattresses for beds, and some cooking-pots. Aziza's family were obviously very poor indeed.

Aziza's mother sat cross-legged on the floor pounding rice into powder in a bowl. She looked up in surprise at the Brownies, but rose and greeted them in the polite Arab manner, welcoming them to her home. Then she took the money which Aziza had earned from selling her flowers, her dark-skinned face lighting up and her brown eyes shining with thankfulness.

"For you, my mother," said little Aziza, with a loving smile.

Leila and Mariam looked at one another and nodded. They took all the flowers they had picked and transferred them to Aziza's basket, heaping it up. She and her mother watched them wide-eyed.

"There, Aziza!" said Leila. "These are all ready for you to sell this afternoon."

"But you said you needed money —" Aziza faltered.

"We said we help other people," Leila reminded her, smiling, "so today we are helping you. Go back to the road this afternoon and you will have all these to sell. And here's what we got for the others," she added, handing it to Aziza's mother.

"Well," said Mariam with a sigh as they made their way back to the road, "that was a bright money-making idea that didn't come off!"

"Oh, *I* think it did!" Leila replied decidedly. "I think it's the best good turn we've ever done!"

PUZZLE CORNER

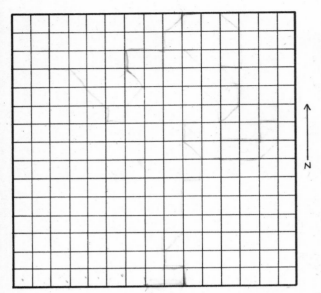

What is it?

TEST your knowledge of the points of the compass with this drawing, using one square for each stroke. Start at the bottom, seven squares in from the left-hand corner, and draw:

Two squares E, 1 N, 1 W, 1 N, 1 NE, 3 N, 1 E, 1 N, 1 NW, 1 N, 1 E, 2 S, 3 E, 1 NE, 1 N, 1 W, 1 S, 2 W, 1 N, 1 NE, 1 N, 1 NW, 1 E, 2 N, 1 NW, 2 W, 1 SW, 1 S, 1 SE, 4 W, 2 SW, 1 S, 1 E, 1 N, 1 NE, 3 E, 1 SW, 1 S, 2 W, 1 S, 1 SE, 1 SW, 1 S, 1 W, 1 N, 2 NW, 1 W, 1 SW, 1 S, 1 E, 1 N, 1 E, 1 S, 2 SE, 1 E, 2 NE, 1 SE, 2 S, 1 SW, 2 S.

WHO?
by Jean Howard

Who bids us be ready
For tasks yet untried
Which we feel are beyond us?
Our own World Chief Guide!

Who knows it is hard
With a pain in our side
To keep right on running?
Our own World Chief Guide!

Who seeks to encourage
With wisdom and pride
The aims of our Movement?
Our own World Chief Guide!

Who sends her good wishes
Throughout the world wide
To all Guides and Brownies?
Our own World Chief Guide!

HO, HO, HO!

Who is given the sack as soon as he starts work?
The postman.

Clerk: There's a salesman outside with a bald head.
Boss: Tell him to go away. I've already got one.

Why is a clock thought to be shy?
Because it always has its hands in front of its face.

THE JEANNETTES OF FRANCE ~

by
Shirley A. Bennett

"Jeannettes" is the name given to Brownies belonging to the Guides de France, one of the four associations which make up Scoutisme Feminin Français, the French National Guide Association.

De Notre Mieux   We Do Our Best

On Sunday morning Fabienne set off to her first meeting with the Jeannettes. She looked very neat in her new uniform—a pale-blue blouse, dark-blue pullover, navy-blue pleated skirt, navy beret and white socks.

When she arrived at the Hut she was greeted by her "Cheftaines" (Brownie Guiders), Isabelle and Karine, and the other Jeannettes of the "Ronde" ("Ronde" means Round, which is what the Pack is called in France).

The Hut, as the Headquarters of the "Ronde" is called, was clean and white, with paintings and decorations on the walls. Isabelle made everyone sit down in a circle, and then she told the newcomers about the Jeannettes.

The Jeannettes were founded in France in 1926 by Marie Diemer. They are called Jeannettes after Jeanne d'Arc (Joan of Arc), who, chosen by God, always did her best to do what was asked of her. Happily, the wars between France and England are past history. The important thing now is that the Brownies and the Jeannettes have the same Motto, the same Law and the same Promise.

I promise that I will do my best
To do my duty
To God,
To France,
To my parents,
To the Law of the Pack,
And to do a good turn every day.

Isabelle explained that their Promise to try to be a real Jeannette was shown by the badge worn on their beret. Their Promise to do their duty to God was shown by wearing His badge, a cross, their Promise badge. Their Promise to do their duty to their country was shown by the badge bearing the arms of their country.

Fabienne felt that all these Promises would be very difficult to keep, but was reassured when Isabelle said that she, Karine and all the other Jeannettes were there to help them. If they decided to become Jeannettes they would enter the Forest and learn the Secrets of the Forest, which would help them to keep the Jeannettes' Law and Promise.

Then the Jeannettes went off to explore Paris

10

for the rest of the day. When Fabienne got home her head was full of everything she had heard and she was impatient for next Sunday to arrive.

Fabienne was quite sure that she wanted to become a Jeannette, and at the next meeting, with five other girls, she entered the Forest. This ceremony was held in the yard outside the Hut. Isabelle and Karine stood at the head; on either side the Sixes made an avenue; and the six new Jeannettes came running from the opposite side of the yard and stood before the Cheftaines. Isabelle asked them if they really wanted to become Jeannettes, and when they all answered "yes" she gave them a booklet called "Towards the Blue Flower" and their Six badges. Fabienne's was white; the others were orange, green and blue.

These are the things Fabienne found she had to learn to do on the First Footpath of the Forest towards her Blue Flower:—

1. Be observant. Use your eyes by finding things in the forest; plant a bulb and watch it grow.
2. Cleanliness. Keep fit—e.g., ball games, skipping.
3. Pray. Learn the Jeannettes' prayer.

A Jeannette makes her Promise

4. Do a good turn every day—e.g., lay the table, clean shoes.
5. Be friendly and polite.
6. Be active with your fingers—e.g., learn some knots and how to address an envelope; make something with scissors and glue.
7. Prepare your own rucksack for outings.
8. Get to know the district where you live.
9. Nature study. How to keep the countryside tidy.
10. Be orderly when out.

The following Sunday Fabienne said the Jeannettes' Promise in a loud voice in front of the Cheftaines, the Pack and her parents, and made the Jeannettes' salute. Isabelle then presented her with her tie, Promise badge, Blue Flower badge and booklet "Towards the White Flower". The things she would learn to do on the Second Footpath are much the same as British Brownies do on the Brownie Road:—

Six new Jeannettes "enter the Forest"

1. Be observant. Look after and observe a plant, animal or insect for 15 days and then return it to the forest.
2. Pray. Go to church every Sunday.
3. Find out what things the Pack does to obey the Law.
4. Cleanliness; keep fit—e.g., gym, swimming.
5. Be gay—e.g., be cheerful at home; decorate your room or the Hut to make it more gay.
6. Learn the songs and dances of the Jeannettes. Do a mime or play. Make a costume.
7. Know how to use the telephone to call the doctor or fire brigade.
8. Know the area where you live and make a map of it.
9. Prepare breakfast or tea; cook a simple meal.
10. Do the shopping.
11. Assist at the "Conseil de Ronde" (Pack's Pow-Wow).
12. Be responsible for some job in the Pack—e.g., look after the plants.
13. Lay a trail. Stalk without being seen. Know three codes.
14. Pitch a tent.
15. Use a knife. Make some installations at camp.
16. Light and tend a fire.
17. Do a good turn every day.

Nathalie was Fabienne's Sixer. She had her Sixer stripes, her Blue Flower and White Flower badges, and now she was on the Third Footpath working for her Gold Flower. In order to help others a Jeannette must know *how* to do things. The Badge Booklet helps her to learn how to do something really well. There are about forty things to choose from, divided into six sections —Worship, Nature, Country, Service to Others, Sport and Handwork. Nathalie was working for her "Bout de Crayon" badge (Pencil Stub—i.e., Artist). So she invited Fabienne and the other

A Cheftaine and a Sixer

Jeannettes of her Six to her house one Wednesday afternoon for a Six meeting (in France children go to school on Saturday morning but have Wednesday afternoon free). She helped them to make stencils and lino-cuts for Christmas cards, and for three hours they all worked hard.

The Jeannettes' Law

At the next meeting the Cheftaines inspected all the cards and then sent the Jeannettes out in pairs with five cards each and instructions to come back only when they had sold them all. It was a wet Sunday, but the Jeannettes were courageous and persevering and by eleven o'clock they were all back in the Hut. In the meantime the Cheftaines had made some hot chocolate. Whilst the Jeannettes drank this they

Jeannettes make Christmas cards

SOME FRENCH JEANNETTE BADGES

Marmiton (House Orderly)

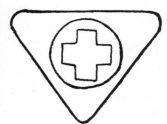 

**Croix-Rouge
(Red Cross)**   **Araignée
(Craft)**

counted the money. The Pack had made over £20, which would be sent to the Guide Headquarters and used to help Jeannettes in Africa.

All the Jeannettes carry a small bag. This contains a notebook and pencil, their booklet, a plastic bag (for collections made in the Forest), string, purse and a clean handkerchief. Fabienne's notebook now contained several dates. The next Saturday was marked AMI D SIX. At first she thought this was a make of car, but it turned out to be an afternoon at the swimming-pool with AMI D SIX—that is to say, Friend *(ami)* of the *(des)* Six. Each Six has a friend, not a member of the Guide Movement, who invites them out somewhere once each term.

After that, in April, there was to be a weekend camp in the Forest of Fontainebleau with all the Jeannettes, Guides, Caravelles, Wolf Cubs, Ran-

gers and Pioneers of the district. The theme was "The Circus" and everyone had to prepare an entertainment for the Camp Fire evening.

Finally in July, Fabienne would attend her first Jeannette camp.

With so many exciting and interesting things to do and discover Fabienne found that, after all, it was not so very difficult learning to say *DE NOTRE MIEUX.*

Isabelle helps the Jeannettes

13

Liechtenstein, Bolivia, Canada and Gibraltar place their
Thinking Day pennies and candles

THINKING

WITH THE 31st and 35th PORTSMOUTH

The Brownies (and a Guide) in the uniforms of many
different countries belonging to the World Association

Photos by

DAY

Austria, Venezuela, the U.S.A., the Netherlands and New Zealand with pennies and candles

BROWNIE GUIDE PACKS

Miss W. J. Beer

Watched by Brownies of the Packs and Guides of the 31st Portsmouth Company, two Guides place their pennies and candles during the ceremony

PUZZLE CORNER

Pan Puzzle

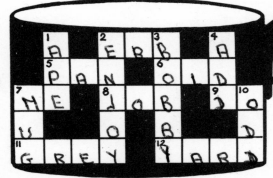

Across

2. The back flow of the tide
5. Shape of this puzzle
6. Not young or middle-aged
7. Yourself
8. Sometimes done as a good turn
9. The opposite of DON'T
11. Colour of sky on a drab day
12. Has three feet, yet can't walk

Down

1. Tailless monkey
2. To delight in
3. Nickname for a policeman
4. To total up
7. You drink from this on Pack holiday
10. Uneven

NATURE TRAIL
Answers to pages 68, 69

1—tree-creeper, 2—linnet, 3—adder, 4—dandelion, 5—lizard, 6—harvest mouse, 7—goat's beard, 8—brimstone butterfly, 9—hare, 10—hedgehog, 11—yellow wagtail, 12—pheasant, 13—slow-worm, 14—primrose, 15—bindweed, 16—red admiral butterfly, 17—partridge, 18—grass-snake, 19—white campion, 20—weasel, 21—thrush, 22—rabbit, 23—skylark, 24—grey squirrel, 25—blackbird, 26—celandine

FIND THE TREASURE
(pages 72, 73)

Middle of sandbank, 7th square from left of p. 73, 13th full square from right

WHAT IS IT?
Solution to puzzle on page 9

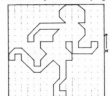

Interest Badge Puzzle
by Daphne M. Pilcher

1. H O S T E S S
2. C Y C L I S T
3. T H R I F T
4. A G I L I T Y
5. T O Y M A K E R
6. B O O K / L O V E R

7. C O O K
8. A R T I S T
9. C R A F T
10. W R I T E R

Hidden in this puzzle are the names of ten Interest badges. To complete the names, write a vowel (a, e, i, o, or u) in each circle and a consonant (one of the other letters) in each square.

16

BROWNIES IN PICTURES

The 1st Paulton (Somerset) Brownie Pack get their *Brownie Annuals* hot from the press. They are standing by the machine on which the annual is printed at the Paulton printing works of Purnell & Sons Ltd.

Colour print by A. Payne

Two 4th Croxley Green (St. Oswald's) Brownies groom a pet dog for the Animal Lover badge. The dog thinks he ought to have the badge!

Colour print by Mrs B. Davis

"There ought to be a badge for cleaning shoes," may well be what the two Brownies from the 1st Billingham (Teesside) Pack are saying, but as they're doing it on Pack holiday it's quite enjoyable!

Colour slide by Mrs J. Heslop

PUZZLE CORNER

SHOP IN THE SUPERMARKET
by Marion Markham

With a pencil trace the correct route round this supermarket in order to spell out a well-known proverb.

You may go across, up or down, but not at a slant, and you must not cross any lines.

Which Badge?
by Marcia M. Armitage

Cross, fly and blanket,
Running, chain, stem;
Why do you think I must
know four of them?
The tray cloth I've made
Also comes in the test.
The badge that I'm taking
I'm sure you'll have guessed.

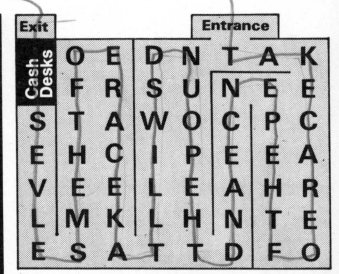

CROSSOUT CROSSWORD
by W. J. Smith

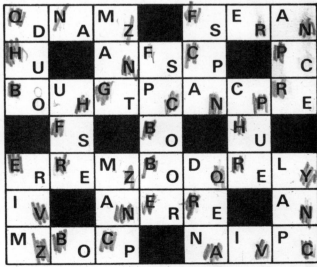

Cross out a letter in each square to leave a finished crossword puzzle.

18

Madurodam

Holland's Tom Thumb Town
by V. Hinton

The tiniest town in the world is in Holland. It is called Madurodam, and it is at The Hague, the city where the Dutch Parliament meets.

Once inside the gates of this "Tom Thumb" town you follow arrows painted on the paths. You wind your way past old and new Dutch buildings only about one-eightieth the size of the real ones, but each one correct in every detail. Everything, including the trees, is in miniature. There are animals as well as people of tiny size in the model town. There are "Tom Thumb" copies of many old Dutch buildings, including the Hall of the Knights, in The Hague. There are old churches, and a Town Hall in which a wedding is taking place. Did you know that Dutch weddings must always be at the Town Hall? If a church wedding is wished for it must take place after the ceremony at the Town Hall.

In Madurodam are modern buildings, as well as old ones—Government offices, a civic centre, and a big secondary school. In one corner is a village fair, and if a one-cent piece is put into a little box everything at the fair begins to work and the music plays. Wander farther along the paths and you come to a recreation ground, with a football stadium, a swimming-pool, cycling and racing tracks, and a boating-pool.

Keep on walking and you reach the docks, with ships moving round the harbour and some being loaded and unloaded. One boat actually catches fire at intervals, and a fire-fighting tender rushes alongside and puts the blaze out with jets of water. It's quite exciting! Near the docks is an airport, with planes taxying along runways and others stationary, with people getting out of them. The planes carry the markings of many different countries.

Going around and across the town is a model railway with a big central station and several smaller ones. As you go round the tiny town, these trains run past. There is a fast transcontinental train, a goods train, and passenger trains. They go over bridges, through cuttings, and along embankments, which are beautifully landscaped and bright with miniature plants.

The town is up to date, for there is a motorway with all kinds of motor transport on it, and there is even a car crash on it with police-car, police, ambulance and ambulance men on the scene.

As this fascinating little town is in Holland, you aren't surprised to see windmills and canals with locks. The last scene is of Dutch bulbfields, with rows and rows of tiny flowers.

If you go to Holland, be sure not to miss visiting Madurodam, the world's tiniest town.

Madurodam

Madurodam, Holland's tiniest town

A square eighty times smaller than the real one

The Hall of the Knights

A Dutch canal on a very small scale

The harbour

Dutch Brownies, who are called Kabouters in Holland

The Town Hall

A miniature motorway

Guides stooping down can still look down on the rooftops

Colour slides by Mrs V. Hinton

Pretty things to make

A GAY NECKLACE

Cut plastic straws of all colours into long and short pieces. Thread these on a long cotton or thread length that will slip easily over your head, and you have a pretty necklace.

by Penny Gaye

A GLITTERING FAN

Cut two semi-circles of thin cardboard, both alike

Glue a lolly-stick to No. 1

Glue No. 2 side in place

Cover both sides with bright foil paper

A circular fan can be made in the same way

You could glue a small mirror to this to add to its charm
Over this glue a paper cake-doiley
Sequins, beads, glitter, etc., can be glued to both sides
of the fan to make it sparkle

A Rose for the Queen

by Anthea A. Muddle

Diana was excited! She cycled home from the Pack meeting bursting with news. Pushing her bike into the garage, she opened the kitchen door. She flung her beret onto a nearby chair, and called out, "Mummy, Mummy, guess what?"

"I'm in here, Diana," answered her mother in a quiet voice from the sitting-room. Mother was sitting quietly, resting. This was the tropical island of Trinidad, and it was hot.

"You know I deliver the papers to Government House on my newspaper round? Well—" Diana took a deep breath—"I'm to take them there while

Diana cycled home in great excitement

the Queen of England is visiting the island. A special detective told our Guider I could."

"That's wonderful news! You'll feel proud. Come and get ready for supper. Did you have a nice meeting?" As she spoke, Diana's mother rose and began to prepare supper.

"Yes," replied Diana. "We were making final plans for our guard-of-honour at the docks when the royal party leave on Monday. Please can I have some new shoes?"

"Please may I," corrected her mother automatically. "You are going to be busy. I'll buy you some new shoes tomorrow. Your brother Brian wants a new film to take pictures of the Scouts and Cubs meeting the Queen."

On Saturday afternoon Diana and the other Brownies joined the Scouts, Cubs and Guides in the brilliant sunshine of the island. There were Negro, Indian, Chinese and European children among them.

Diana glanced up at the two flags flying together, the red-white-and-blue of the Union Flag alongside the new West Indian one of her own island. Suddenly she heard

24

cheers in the distance. She stood very still as the royal car approached slowly. She wished the driver would stop. She wanted to have a good long look at the Queen. With all the other Brownies, Guides, Cubs and Scouts, she saluted as the car passed. She thought the Queen actually smiled at her!

"She seems small to be such an important person," she said to herself.

All too soon it was over. The Troops, Companies and Packs were dismissed. Diana hurried home. At supper Brian was talking about the pictures he had taken. No one remarked that Diana was very quiet. Her mother decided that she was tired from all the excitement.

"Diana, you have to be up early tomorrow to deliver your papers. You should have an early night," she said.

"Yes, I have to collect them first. I do hope it doesn't rain." Diana's face fell at the awful thought.

"Duffer!" laughed Brian kindly. "It won't rain. If it does I'll run you to the newsagent's in Dad's car."

The two children looked at their father. He smiled and said, "The Queen is certainly disrupting our household! First my camera disappears; now my car!" There was a twinkle in his dark eyes.

She cut a red rose still wet with dew

She rode off, holding the rose with great care

Diana's mother and father were white West Indians. They were quite well off, but Diana did a newspaper round to earn herself pocket-money.

That night she lay awake thinking. She longed to give the Queen a gift. But how could she do it? She was just one girl among the thousands who would see the Queen. And what could she give the Queen, who must surely have everything she needed?

Then suddenly, thinking of her own small possessions and then of her family's, inspiration came. A rose—a beautiful rose from the garden!

Next morning Diana rose very early and put on her Brownie uniform. She didn't usually wear uniform when she delivered newspapers, but this was a very special occasion! The sun was shining as she stole out into the garden. Very carefully, she cut one perfect rose. It was a beautiful red, and still covered with dew.

"Mummy, I'm going to give the Queen a rose. Do you think she would like one?" she asked anxiously when her mother came downstairs.

"Yes, I'm sure she would, especially as

it is your very own idea. I'll give you some cellophane and a pin." Her mother took the rose, and Diana wrote on a clean piece of paper *To the Queen from her newspaper girl, Diana.* As an afterthought, she added her name and address and the name of her Brownie Guide Pack.

Her mother waved goodbye as she set off on her important errand, holding the rose very carefully. The big iron gates at the entrance to the drive into Government House stood open. Two soldiers were on guard in front of their sentry boxes. Diana felt a little nervous as she cycled past them to the gatehouse.

A kind-looking policeman came out to her. "Your name, young lady?" he asked in a deep voice.

"Diana, sir. I've brought the Queen's newspapers."

The policeman noticed the rose. "What's this, a rose? What a beauty! For the Queen, is it? Well, I don't know." He scratched his head and continued, "Anyway, go along to the side door, and ring the bell. Give the newspapers to the doorman there."

"Oh, you must be Diana!"

Diana cycled up the wide drive

Diana cycled up the wide drive between the tropical palm-trees lining it that provided both shade and privacy for the tall old building. She had been inside once before, when, soon after the island became independent, it became a museum and the public were allowed in to see the beautiful furniture and pictures. For this royal visit the house had been cleaned and refurnished and draped with flags.

"Will the Queen really get my rose?" Diana asked the doorman.

"Yes, it will go on Her Majesty's breakfast tray." The doorman smiled at the Brownie's anxious face. "I promise you I'll see that it does."

Diana went away satisfied.

That afternoon she was playing in the garden when a large black car drew up. A lady alighted and came towards her.

"I am one of the Queen's ladies-in-waiting. I have come to see the girl who delivers newspapers. Oh, you must be Diana, who sent the Queen a rose!"

Diana nodded. She could hardly speak.

"Her Majesty sent me to give you her special thanks. She was very touched at your kind thought. Here is a personal letter for you." The lady smiled and handed Diana a letter.

"Th-thank you," stammered Diana. She could hardly believe it had all happened even as she watched the lady return to the car, which was driven swiftly away.

She dashed indoors. "Daddy, Mummy, Brian, look at this! I've got a letter from the Queen!" Proudly she held up the short letter, which bore the royal coat-of-arms and the signature of the Queen.

When the family had got over the surprise and excitement they all felt at Diana's news, Brian said: "I'll give you one of my pictures of the royal visit, Diana, and you can mount your letter with it."

"Please may I go and show our Guider and the other Brownies, Mum?" asked Diana.

Her mother nodded. "Of course!"

Diana's father drove her to the Brownie Guider's house. Most of the island was on holiday for the royal visit, so the Guider was at home.

"You must be feeling very proud, Diana," she said. "I know that the whole Pack will be when they hear about it. Perhaps one day you will become a Queen's Guide."

"I hope so," said Diana. "After this, when I go up to Guides, I shall work to be one."

On the way back home Diana said to her father, "If I do become a Queen's Guide, I shall write to the Queen and tell her that I was once her newspaper girl."

"Look at this! I've got a letter from the Queen!"

UNION FLAG Jigsaw Game
A Game for You to Make and Play

by Daphne Pilcher

Making this game will remind you how the Union Flag is made up of the red cross of St. George against a white ground, the white cross of St. Andrew against a blue ground, and the red cross of St. Patrick against a white ground.

To play it you will need a FLAG CARD and a complete set of the flag parts for each player and a dice and a shaker between you.

TO MAKE: Take a piece of white card 216mm ($8\frac{1}{2}''$) by 140mm ($5\frac{1}{2}''$) and mark it as the Union Flag.

From a red card cut one of each of Diagrams 2 and 3 and two of each of Diagrams 4 and 5.

From a blue card cut two of Diagram 6a, two of Diagram 6b, two of Diagram 7a and two of Diagram 7b. If your blue card is a different colour on the back you will have to cut another of each of the shapes of Diagrams 6a, 6b, 7a and 7b.

TO PLAY: Each player shakes the dice in turn. As soon as a player has thrown a six she may take up her flag card. As she throws a number she may then pick up a numbered piece and place it on the card in the correct place. Only one piece may be picked up for each throw. The winner is the player who completes her flag first.

The Union Flag is shown opposite.

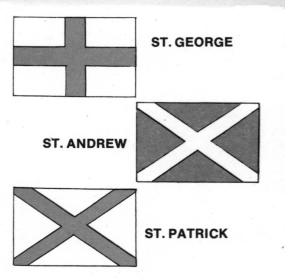

ST. GEORGE

ST. ANDREW

ST. PATRICK

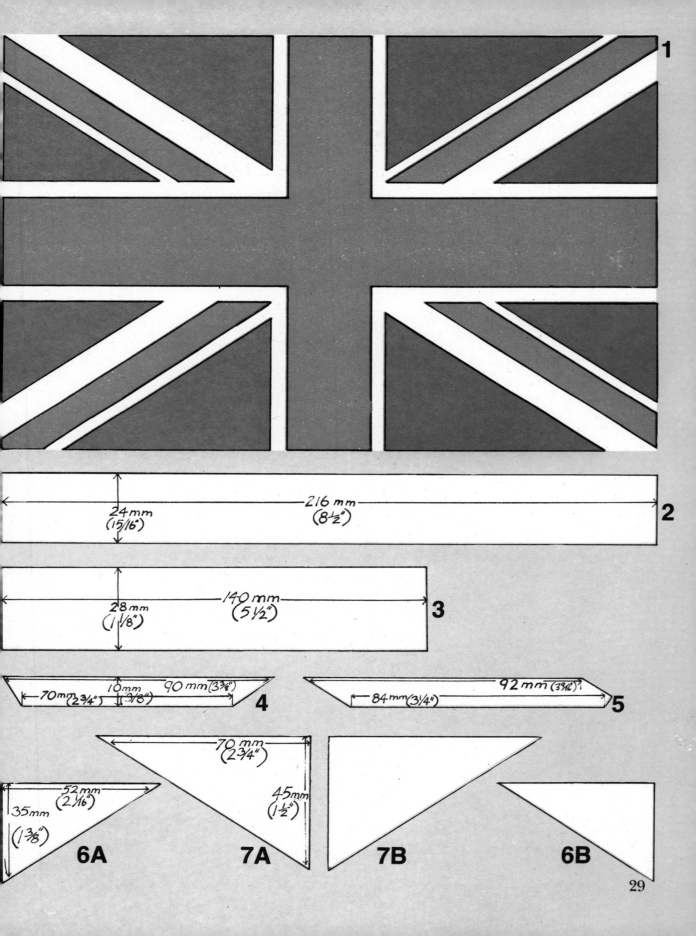

1

2 — 216 mm (8½") / 24 mm (15/16")

3 — 140 mm (5½") / 28 mm (1⅛")

4 — 70 mm (2¾") / 10 mm (3/8") / 90 mm (3⅜")

5 — 92 mm (3⅞") / 84 mm (3¼")

6A — 52 mm (2 1/16") / 35 mm (1⅜")

7A — 70 mm (2¾") / 45 mm (1½")

7B

6B

OUR PACK HOLIDAY

by Marcia M. Armitage

1. Pack Holiday started one hot August day,
And we laughed, joked and sang every bit of the way.
The house we would live in was terribly old,
And in spite of the sunshine was dark, damp and cold.

2. Brown Owl lit a fire to dispel the gloom
While we all unpacked and explored every room.
When supper was over we climbed in our beds
With Brownie songs still ringing in our heads.

3. On Sunday, the chores done, to church
    we all hurried,
Then wrote letters home in case parents were worried.
We went for a Nature walk; this was when Kate
Fell into a bog. Gosh, she was in a state!

4. Monday it thundered and lightened and rained,
So we did handcrafts with team points to be gained.
I painted a portrait of Melanie Brown,
But it looked a lot better when viewed upside-down.

30

5. On Tuesday we hiked, though it rained all the while,
But as Brownies should we remembered to smile,
Then back at the house we each had a hot shower,
With cocoa in bed at a rather late hour.

6. Wednesday brought visitors streaming to camp;
The sun blazing down had soon dried up the damp.
We served tea and biscuits and proudly displayed
The games we had learnt and the things we had made.

8. On Friday we made up and acted a play,
For it rained once again on this our last day.
Brown Owl brought cakes, apples, drinks, and said
We could have a small pre-midnight feast in our bed.

7. On Thursday to shop in the village we went,
And on gifts to take home all our money we spent.
We baked potatoes at night, but Belinda
Forgot about hers and it came out a cinder.

9. On Saturday we made the house neat and clean
So that no one could see any dirt where we'd been;
Then back to our homes we all wended our way
With most happy thoughts of our Pack Holiday.

My hat!

Plymouth Brownies hike over Dartmoor in unusual "hats"—made of ferns—to keep the sun from their heads

Colour print by Miss E. A. Roper

This is the 19th High Wycombe's (St. Mark's) winning entry, "Pack Flower Border", in a novel competition at High Wycombe's District Brownie Revels

Colour print by Miss S. Ball

The 2nd Epping Pack create a delightful variety of unusual and charming hats on Pack holiday

Colour print by Mrs R. Cuthbert

Not so much hats as heads disguise these 1st Aylsham (Norwich) Ranger "dwarfs", visiting Brownies on Pack holiday

Colour slide by Mrs E. Seeley

Brownies of the 1st, 2nd and 3rd Aylsham Packs put on animal heads and bodies (and sometimes tails!) to take part in the local carnival

Colour slide by Mrs E. Seeley

PACK!

BY JEAN HOWARD

Brownie Revels, having fun,
Shouting to the Sixer, "RUN!"
What a noise! Well, never mind!
Come on, Gnomes, you're left behind!
Yet no one speaks or answers back
When Brownie Guider calls out "PACK!"

Sometimes Brownies rush around,
Playing "Touch!" or "Feet Off Ground".
At Pow-wow time they tell their news,
Suggest ideas, air their views;
But no one speaks or answers back
When Brownie Guider calls out "Pack!"

Sing and laugh and rush about,
Chase each other in and out;
Elves and Pixies, chatter, chatter,
Imps and Kelpies, clatter, clatter!
Yet no one speaks or answers back
When Brownie Guider calls out "Pack!"

— c

Barbara's Christmas Service

A short short story by Jean Howard

Barbara polished her badge and shoes and ironed her tie ready for the District Carol Service in the afternoon.

Her Brownie Guider had asked if she would like to read one of the lessons, but her legs began to feel like jelly at the very thought of standing up in front of all the Guiders and Brownies, so she'd asked for Judy to do it instead.

The church seemed full of the atmosphere of Christmas, with candlelight and flowers and evergreens and a tall Christmas tree that nearly touched the ceiling. Beneath the tree the crib glowed softly near the chancel steps.

The church was decorated for the carol service

Barbara slipped into her place at the end of the front row and sat quietly while the church filled with people in brown and blue uniforms.

Marie, a handicapped Guide, was wheeled up to the front by the crib so that she could lead the renewal of the Promise, and then the service began with the lovely carol "Silent night".

After a prayer, Judy walked up to the lectern to read the first lesson. In a clear voice she began to read the age-old words, "And there were in the same country shepherds abiding in the fields . . ."

Then it happened!

One of the candles suddenly slipped sideways, hung there for a moment, and then fell down on to the straw spread around the outside of the crib. Within seconds the straw blazed up and caught the edge of the lowest branch of the Christmas tree. This was as dry as tinder, and a wicked yellow flame leapt upwards, licking at the branch above.

Marie screamed with fear and held up her arms to protect her face from the heat of the flames. Quick as thought,

Barbara jumped up and pushed the wheelchair out of danger

Barbara jumped into the aisle and gave the wheelchair a push, which sent it rolling backwards out of harm's way. Barbara grabbed a large vase full of Michaelmas daisies that was standing on the stone floor. Pulling the flowers out as she ran, she threw the water over the blazing straw and branches. About as quickly as it had flared up, the fire went out. The danger was past.

The whole episode was over so quickly that many at the back of the church hardly realised that anything was amiss, but the Guiders in the front and the minister, who had leapt forward to help, knew how effective Barbara's quick action had been. It had saved the handicapped Guide from being harmed.

The only damage caused was a mess of charred straw, some singed branches, and a large pool of black water on the floor.

"Thank you," the minister murmured to Barbara as she took her seat again.

The service continued with the carol "Hark the Herald Angels Sing". No one sang it more joyfully than Barbara, for she had proved to herself that even if she was nervous of reading the lesson in public she wasn't scared to act in an emergency.

PUZZLE CORNER

Cup Crossword Puzzle

by Helen N. Martindale

CLUES ACROSS
4. Do you know this code?
5. These sail on the sea

CLUES DOWN
1. To break violently
2. You may follow this sometimes
3. Four-footed animal

Cookery Signpost Puzzle

by M. J. Eckhardt

Clues
1) The top of the milk
2) Fruit, often used in pies
3) A sweetener, either white or brown in colour
4) Insides of poultry—useful as stock
5) Dried fruit of the grape
6) Vegetable used in summer salads
7) Large prawns
8) A spice grated on sweets for added flavour
9) Very small fish—sold in tins

If clues are answered correctly, the word down the signpost is the name of a cooking fat.

Can You Solve This?

If a frog at the bottom of a well forty feet deep jumps up three feet every day, but at night falls back two, how many days will he need to get right out of the well?

When the Clock Strikes Twelve

A Play for Brownies to Read and Act
by Delphine Evans

Characters

Clock (circle of cardboard around face, showing midnight. Gong to strike)
Toy Soldier   Golliwog
Two Christmas Fairies,
1 white, 1 pink
Jack-in-the-Box (large box with lid closed)
Bride Doll   Robot
Doll in a Box (tied by arms and legs into box)
Teddy Bear
Sailor Doll (to be wrapped in parcel on stage. One button on his suit is missing)

Extras (any number—can be dressed as soft toys or wear a cardboard box painted a bright colour for building-bricks)
Jack-in-the-Box and Sailor Doll: It is suggested that these two characters should have the side of the box facing back stage open, so that they can stay inside until they appear

Scene

A toyshop with the toys displayed neatly. Parcel with Sailor Doll inside in prominent position. As the curtain rises the toys are standing perfectly still. The clock strikes twelve and they come alive. Bride Doll starts to cry. During the performance the hands on the clock should be moved gradually to three o'clock.

GOLLY: I thought twelve o'clock would never come. Someone twisted my foot as they put me back on the shelf and I've been standing crooked ever since. I was afraid I'd fall off *(straightens himself)*. That's better.

SOLDIER: Thank goodness you're not crying about it. That stupid Bride Doll has been crying for days now.

GOLLY: Well, it was all your fault, Soldier Boy, because you told her you didn't want to marry her.

SOLDIER: I'm not going to marry her now. She only wants me because Sailor Doll has been sold.

(Bride Doll starts crying louder)

GOLLY: Oh, please don't mention the word "Sailor"; it only starts her off again.

SOLDIER: If she had said yes the first time I asked her, everything would have been all right.

PINK FAIRY: I wish you two would stop arguing. I'm beginning to wish someone would come and buy you. Now come along! Let me see you smile and make up.

(Soldier and Golly shake hands and smile)

PINK FAIRY: That's better. Now what shall we do? Three o'clock will soon be here and our magic time will be gone.

WHITE FAIRY: Let's open this parcel. I wonder where it came from.

GOLLY: We don't want to bother with that now.

PINK FAIRY: That can wait. Let's play some games.

WHITE FAIRY: It seems very quiet tonight. Has anyone been sold today?

PINK FAIRY: No, I don't think so. No one has gone since Sailor Doll.

BRIDE *(sniff, sniff)*: Please try not to mention him. I feel so unhappy every time I hear his name.

PINK FAIRY: I'm sorry, Bride Doll. But you really must stop all this crying. There are plenty of other dolls you can marry.

BRIDE: Soldier doesn't want me. Golly doesn't want me, and Jack-in-the-Box is broken.

WHITE FAIRY: For goodness' sake stop! Perhaps someone will come and buy you soon. We poor fairies have got to stay here until next Christmas. No one wants us except for the top of the tree, and we don't mind.

PINK FAIRY: What about poor old Jack-in-the-Box? His spring is broken and he can't even get out of his box. Just think about him!

(Soldier walks across to Jack)

SOLDIER: I think he was mended today. Shall I open him and see?

(Golly goes to help)

GOLLY: Yes, I'll help you. He's such a happy fellow.

(Both undo the latch, and Jack jumps up)

JACK: Hello! Hello! How do you do! I'm mended now and just like new. Jump up and down—be just like me *(appropriate actions)*—I'm mended now—I'm so *happee—ee!*

SOLDIER: Hello, Jack! It is nice to see you again. What happened to you?

JACK: My spring was twisted, then went pop. Inside my box I had to stop.

BRIDE: Poor, poor Jack! Are you better now? *(walks across to him)*

JACK: Of course I am—can't you see? I'm mended now—I'm so happee—ee.

BRIDE: I'm so pleased. I've missed you such a lot.

GOLLY: Oh, don't listen to her. She's got the miseries. You'd better be careful; she's looking for someone to marry.

SOLDIER: Golly and I don't want her. You can have her, Jack.

BRIDE: He is rather sweet. I never really looked at him before.

JACK: Oh, no, my dear—I cannot marry you. There's no room in my box for two.

(Bride starts crying again)

DOLL IN BOX: Please stop crying. Think how lucky you are to be able to walk. I'm tied in my box and can't play games or anything.

PINK FAIRY: Yes, that's right and she is always smiling. Look how pretty she is. Everyone loves her.

BRIDE: Well, she's not all dressed up to be married.

TEDDY BEAR: It's no good, I can't stand this noise any longer. We will have to find someone for her to marry.

WHITE FAIRY: What about Robot? He's very quiet tonight.

GOLLY: I'll go and see what's the matter with him. *(As he walks across he trips over the parcel.)* We shall have to move this parcel out of the way in a minute.

SOLDIER *(looking at parcel)*: I wonder what *is* inside it?

DOLL IN BOX: It's only a brown paper parcel. I expect it's a new toy that's been delivered.

GOLLY: Never mind that now. Let's see what is the matter with Robot.

SOLDIER *(poking and prodding Robot)*: He's standing up, but he seems to be asleep. Let's try pushing him.

(Soldier and Golly try to push him, but he does not move)

JACK: Just take a look—it's clear to see. Turn him around—you will find a key. Now wind him up—he'll come to life. But I really don't think he wants a wife.

(They wind him up and he walks stiffly and speaks jerkily)

ROBOT: Thank—you—kind—friends. Now—I—can—move—again.

DOLL IN BOX: Do you want someone to marry you, Robot?

ROBOT: I—do—not—compute. What—does—marry—mean?

GOLLY: Oh, never mind that now. I can't wait any longer to see what is inside this box. Who is going to help me unwrap it?

FAIRIES AND SOLDIER: We will *(all go to help and start unwrapping. Bride Doll stands and watches).*

SOLDIER: It's wrapped up extremely well.

GOLLY: Pull that string. It's nearly open now. Good gracious!

(Everyone stands back as Sailor Doll comes out of parcel)

SAILOR: Thank you, friends, for unwrapping me.

BRIDE: *(going to him and holding his hand)*: It's my Sailor—come back to me.

GOLLY: Whatever were you doing in that parcel? We all thought you had been sold.

SAILOR: Yes, I was. But the lady who bought me noticed that I had a button missing, so she exchanged me for a book.

BRIDE: I'm so pleased you are back. When we are married I will sew your button on for you.

SOLDIER: Look at the time! It's almost three o'clock. We must hurry back into our places and tidy ourselves before the clock strikes.

(All run to their original places, Bride Doll and Sailor holding hands. The clock strikes three and they are immediately still)

CURTAIN

VENTURES AND CHALLENGES

Brownies think of lots of interesting and exciting things to do.

Some of the 14th Halifax (All Saints) passed the Outdoor Challenge for the Brownie Road by making potato men. They cut the tops of the potatoes off, scooped out the centres, and put in wet cotton-wool with bird-seed on it. Then they cut out paper faces and added matchstick "legs". They watered the seed, and after a few weeks it grew like hair.

The 3rd Ringwood Pack had a Christmas Pudding Venture. All the Brownies brought different items for the pudding—eggs, sultanas, suet, sugar, flour, spice, etc. All the mixture was put into one big bowl. Each Brownie stirred it and made a wish. A number of Brownies brought along basins, and altogether twenty lovely Christmas puddings were made. The Brownies took them round to old people, who much appreciated them.

For their "Brownies Are Friendly" Challenge for the Highway badge, Brownies of another Pack dressed dolls in the uniforms of Norway, Japan, Australia and the U.S.A. This gave another Brownie the idea of Lending a Hand by making a base for the dolls to stand on. Two other

songs of the four countries round the dressed dolls.

The 2nd Pyrford Pack, Surrey, had a very interesting idea. They held an Olympic meeting indoors. Each Six chose a country to represent and made its flag. Then they competed in various events. The winners mounted

Brownies who were working for the Footpath badge joined in and painted pictures of scenes in the four countries. Another Brownie wrote out the Brownie Promise inside the shape of the Brownie badge, and when Thinking Day came all the Brownies sang

a box and received a gold "medal", which was really a chocolate in gold paper. When a Six was awarded a "medal" its flag was raised. The District Commissioner presented the prizes, which went to Japan, Australia and Russia.

The day everything went wrong

by Barbara Thomas

Crash! The cup of tea Valerie was carrying slid off the saucer and broke into dozens of pieces.

"Whatever are you doing up there, Val?" Mummy called up the stairs. She sounded cross.

"I was only trying to do a good turn and take Granny a cup of tea in bed," faltered Valerie, gazing in dismay at the scalding tea soaking .nto the carpet.

Mummy came running up the stairs. "It was kind of you to think of taking Granny a cup of tea," she said, "but you shouldn't have tried to carry a plate of biscuits as well. Now go and get a cloth, and let's clear up all this mess."

Miserably Valerie obeyed. What a way to start the day! Just when she wanted to do everything right and show Mummy what a good Brownie she was, too! The Brownie Guider was planning a Pack holiday for the Brownies this summer, and Valerie was dying to go. It was the first time there'd been a chance, and next year she would be going up to Guides, and would be too old. Mummy hadn't quite decided whether to let her go yet, so Valerie wanted to show her how grown-up and sensible she could be.

"I'll just have to think of something

The cup of tea slid from the saucer

else," she thought, wandering out into the garden.

There she had a really good idea. She would clean out the guinea-pigs' hutches. She was working for her Animal Lover badge, and had already looked after her guinea-pig, Florence, for nearly three months. Today she would be extra helpful and clean out Dougal's hutch as well. Dougal belonged to her big brother, Peter; he had got his name because he was the long-haired Peruvian kind and looked just like Dougal of TV's "Magic Roundabout".

Valerie liked it in the guinea-pigs' shed. It was quiet there and smelt of the fresh hay they had for their bedding. Florence and Dougal welcomed her excitedly as usual, whistling loudly and pressing their funny little noses against the wire-netting. Valerie lifted Florence out and put her in a cardboard box with some fresh grass while she cleaned out her cage. First she took out the food-dish and water-bottle and washed them; then she shovelled out all the soiled sawdust and pellets from the run and sleeping quarters, sprinkled fresh sawdust on the floor, and put some hay in the bedroom. After this, she filled Florence's dish with food, and put fresh water in her bottle. All this time, Florence stayed contentedly in her box, nibbling away at the grass. When the cage was ready for her, Valerie lifted her back in, and she trotted round every corner, snuffling excitedly, as though she was saying "thank you".

Now it was Dougal's turn. Peter *would* be pleased when he found out what she had done, thought Valerie, as she lifted Dougal into the box. But Dougal had other ideas. The moment Valerie turned her back he jumped out of the box. The next thing she knew, he had run behind a sack of peat in the corner of the shed.

"Oh, dear, whatever will Peter say?" thought poor Valerie, trying to grab Dougal.

She soon found that he could move a lot faster than she could. Each time she thought she'd got her hands round him he managed to slip away, and soon the shed was in a dreadful mess, with peat, garden tools and hay all over the place, and Dougal still free, chattering his teeth in the corner. Just then, who should come

The guinea-pig escaped into a corner

through the door but Peter!

"Whatever have you been doing in here, Val?" he said, taking in the scene at a glance. "Poor old Dougal looks frightened to death!"

Valerie felt like bursting into tears. "I was going to give you a surprise," she began but Peter cut in.

"You've done that all right! Now go and see if you can find a few dandelion leaves."

Valeria did as she was told, and was soon back.

Peter put them in a box that he tipped on one side. In a moment Dougal ran into it and was soon munching happily.

"That's the way to catch guinea-pigs," said Peter in a superior voice. "They only run faster if you keep chasing them. Now clear off, kid. I'll see to Dougal myself."

Valerie slunk away. Here was another good turn gone wrong, and Peter had made her feel really small! "I'll put my uniform on ready for Brownies," she decided. After that, she wandered gloomily down to the bottom of the garden, and gazed over the fields stretching beyond. These were called "small-holdings" because they weren't as big as proper farms. The people who owned them each had a bit of land with a few cows, some chickens, and maybe a pig or two; they mostly had other jobs as well. Valerie's best friend in Brownies, Enid Wilson, lived on one of the small-holdings, and Valerie could just see her house through the trees. She was going on the Pack holiday, and this was partly why Valerie was so keen to go too.

Enid's father was out in his fields today, driving a tractor pulling a machine that gathered up the loose hay in some rollers, and then shot it out shaped into neatly-packed blocks. Valerie stood watching him. She wondered whether to go and call for Enid, but there were cows in one of the fields between, and whenever she called for Enid she always went the long way round by the road because of those cows. Enid always laughed at her, and so did Peter, but it was no good; Valerie always thought the cows were just waiting for a chance to chase her; what they would do when they caught her she didn't dare think about!

Watching Mr Wilson helped Valerie forget how everything had been going wrong today. She was surprised to hear Peter's voice close behind her.

"There'll be lots of hay left for the guinea-pigs," he said, sounding pleased.

Valerie nodded. Mr Wilson always let them glean the hay that was left behind by the machine, and there was usually plenty.

"We filled six sacks last year, didn't we?" she said. "They gobbled it all up, too, by the end of the winter."

"Well, Florence had two litters last year, so we had a lot to feed."

"I wish Mum had let us keep some of them."

"Never mind. She said we could put Florence and Dougal together again soon, and then we'll have some more babies."

"Enid will be sure to want one of them," said Valerie. "She told me hers is lonely because he's on his own."

"Well, I'm going for a ride on my bike now," stated Peter. "There's nothing to do here. Granny's having a snooze, and Mum's gone down to the shop."

"Go on, then. I'm going to stay here and watch Mr Wilson."

"Mum won't be long. Don't go near Dougal, whatever you do." With this parting shot Peter went.

It was very peaceful leaning over the fence watching Enid's daddy working. The tractor made a sort of purring noise. Every now and then the sound changed as Mr Wilson stopped to get off and rake up the hay or to free the rollers when they became clogged. Usually there was a man to help him with these jobs, but he seemed to be on his own this afternoon.

He'd done most of the field now and was just approaching the little bank at the bottom end. He must have left this until last because it was awkward, thought Val. There were one or two trees growing there, and the ground sloped steeply. The sound of the tractor changed again, and to Valerie's horror it tipped over on the slope!

Mr Wilson was thrown off. The tractor seemed to be falling on top of him, but at the last moment it caught against a tree. Valerie could just see Mr Wilson lying on the ground, but he didn't seem to be moving.

She could never remember climbing the fence and running through the hay-field, but she must have done, for the next thing she knew she was gazing down at Mr Wilson. His leg seemed to be

To Valerie's horror, the tractor tipped over, throwing Mr Wilson off

trapped beneath the tractor. Valerie could hardly bear to look at him, his face was so grey and queer-looking. He opened his eyes and tried to speak.

"Get help!" he whispered hoarsely. "Can you . . . try to . . . switch the engine off?" Then he fainted.

Valerie looked doubtfully at the tractor. The throb of the engine was making it rock dangerously. It didn't look very safe balanced against the tree, and if it fell it would crash right onto Mr Wilson. She could see a key in the dashboard, and it was just within her reach. Nervously she turned it. The engine stopped at once.

What should she do now? She knew what she wanted to do—race back home as fast as her trembling legs would carry her. But there was nobody at home! She would have to go on through the fields and tell Mrs Wilson what had happened. What about those awful cows, though? How could she possibly face them? For a moment she hesitated, then Mr Wilson

gave a groan, and that decided her. Cows or no cows, she had to get help before the tractor fell on Mr Wilson.

She hurried through the gate into the next field. This was another hayfield, and she ran quickly around the edge until she came to the gate leading to the field with the cows. There they were, about a dozen of them, big black-and-white ones— Friesians, she thought Enid called them. Trying not to think about the cows, Valerie slipped into the field and started edging her way down towards the Wilsons' house. She was getting nearer the cows now, and began to go more slowly. Several of the cows had calves with them, and they all seemed to find Valerie very interesting. They turned and stared at her with big, brown eyes. Only the thought of Mr Wilson made Valerie force her quaking legs forward. One of the cows gave a loud "Moo!" and some of the others joined in. That cow had horns—perhaps it wasn't a cow at all but a bull! At this thought Valerie took to her heels and raced the

Valerie dashed to the phone-box and dialled

last few yards past the cows into the safety of the Wilsons' back garden. Panting, she flung herself at the back door.

"Enid! Mrs Wilson!" she cried. "Come quickly!"

There was no reply. Desperately Valerie opened the door. She went in, still calling, but all was quiet, and she suddenly remembered Enid telling her that her mother was taking her shopping this afternoon.

She ran back into the garden, but there was no one in sight. The hens came clucking around her feet, but they weren't any help. Surely she hadn't braved the cows for nothing!

Despairingly, she gazed down the road. There was no sign of Mrs Wilson and Enid, but she realised that she was staring straight at a public telephone box! One of the Challenges on the Brownie Road was to telephone from a public call-box.

Valerie knew just how to do it, but she didn't have any money with her now. What was it the Brownie Guider had told them about using the phone if there was an accident or if the house was on fire? Of course! It was called an emergency call, and you just dialled 999 without putting any money in the coin-box.

Valerie dashed to the phone box. She seized the receiver. Carefully she dialled the three nines and heard it ringing.

"Emergency," replied a distant voice. "Which service, please?"

Valerie's mouth went dry and she couldn't speak.

"Which service do you want?" repeated the voice.

Valerie swallowed hard. "I don't know," she said, "but Mr Wilson's had an accident, and his tractor's fallen on his leg, and he's fainted, and will you please send help straight away?"

"What number are you speaking from?" asked the voice.

Valerie looked at the round disc in the centre of the telephone dial.

"Southfield 339," she said.

"I'll put you through to the ambulance service," replied the voice, and in a moment Valerie was pouring out her story to an ambulance man. "I'm in the telephone box in Green Hayes Lane," she said. "It's the third turning to the left off the main road from Hanbury."

"Thank you very much," said the ambulance man. "Those are very clear directions. We'll be along straight away, and I'll get in touch with the police as well. We may need their help to shift the tractor. Will you wait by the telephone box and show us exactly where to find Mr Wilson?"

"Yes," whispered Valerie, suddenly feeling rather weak.

The next five minutes passed very slowly, but then there was the sound of a siren, and the ambulance arrived, closely followed by a police car.

Everything seemed to happen at once after that. Mr Wilson was released from the tractor, put on a stretcher and gently carried to the ambulance. Then he was whisked off to hospital, and the policemen gave Valerie a lift back home in the police car.

Peter ran out and stared in astonishment and envy when he saw her arrive, but all Valerie wanted was to find her mummy.

"Oh, Mummy," she sobbed, throwing herself into her mother's arms, "I was so frightened, and I did wish you were with me."

When Mummy had finally sorted the whole story out she gave Valerie a big hug and said, "I think you've been a very brave girl. You did your best even though you were frightened, and I'm sure I couldn't have done any better myself."

Later that night when Valerie was tucked up in bed, her mother came in to kiss her goodnight.

"I've just had a chat with Enid's mother," she said. "Mr Wilson's getting on very well in hospital. He's broken his leg, but that will get better quite soon, thanks to you. If you hadn't called for help so quickly he might have been injured really badly. I'm proud of you, Val, and Daddy and I have decided to let you go on the Pack holiday now that you've shown us what a sensible girl you can be."

"Goody!" murmured Valerie, snuggling down under the bedclothes. "I thought everything was going wrong this morning, but it's all come right in the end, after all!"

Valerie saw the men release Mr Wilson and carry him to the ambulance

PUZZLE CORNER

WHICH GUIDE PATROL?

When you go up to Guides which Patrol will you be in? Imagine it's the one shown in this jigsaw. To find out which it is, draw or trace the picture in each frame on the left into the blank frame on the right with the same number; then see if you can name the Patrol.

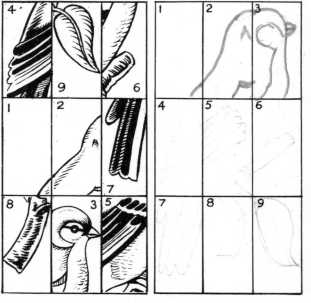

HO, HO, HO!

Twice the people of London have been taken in by the same April Fool joke. But as it was nearly two hundred years after it had first been tried it is not strange that it was easy to take people in a second time.

This second occasion happened nearly a hundred years ago. Many people then were surprised to receive an invitation to attend "the annual ceremony of washing the white lions at the Tower of London". Hundreds of people arrived at the Tower, only to be greeted with the cry of "April Fool!"

RIDDLE-ME-REE

What is the difference between a schoolgirl doing homework and a farmer looking after his cattle?
One is stocking her mind and the other is minding his stock.
Why is a pig never ill?
Because he has to be killed before he is cured.
What did the big chimney say to the little chimney?
You're too young to smoke.
What is the difference between a duck with one wing and a duck with two?
A difference of a pinion.
Which of two flies on a door is angry?
The one that flies off the handle.

BABS AND HER BALLOON

A Comedy in Pictures and Verse

by Olive Phillips

Going to Brownies Babs was stuck,
"A traffic jam, that's just my luck!"

"Perhaps my dad could make me wings,
Because he's always inventing things."

"Couldn't you make me something to fly
Over the roads and up in the sky?"

In his workshop, pondered Dad,
"That's an idea! That's not bad!"

"Let's have a ride, Babs—please let me!"
"One at a time—first, Melanie."

The balloon rose up light and free,
But landed the Brownie in a tree.

"I will not have this bother and fuss,
You'll make a laughing-stock of us."

Soon he had made a motor balloon.
"To take you to Brownies—not to the moon!"

Dad taught Babs all she had to know—
To stop, to start, go high, go low.

After a practice run or two
Babs learned all she had to do.

"Go to Brownies. Keep quite cool.
Go straight there—no playing the fool!"

Over the Guide hall young Babs flew.
"Now I've got a balloon's-eye view!"

Down below the girls all clustered,
Open-mouthed, excited, flustered.

Brown Owl saw their consternation,
"Please give me an explanation!"

"Hello, Brown Owl! Please mind your head!"
Babs parked the balloon by the cycle shed.

On a day of rain and gloom—
Brown Owl's about to leave her room.

"I thought I felt some spots of rain.
There must be a leak in the roof again."

"Take it away, right out of my sight.
Fancy a Brownie flying by kite!"

So Babs went back to riding her bike.
"I'm held up by traffic, which I don't like!"

She clambered through a high trap-door.
"Some slates have fallen off, I'm sure."

She reached the roof, the trap-door slammed.
"What can I do? The door has jammed!"

She tried, her face turned very pale,
The Brownies down below to hail!

51

They telephoned the fire-brigade.
"Come quickly, please! We need your aid!"

"The road is blocked by a fallen tree
And the river is rising rapidly."

"I'm going home for my balloon.
Tell Brown Owl I'll be back quite soon."

Home rushed Babs, stumbling and splashing,
With the wind and the rain around her lashing.

Back to Brown Owl in a gale of force.
"I hope I can keep the balloon on course."

"Brown Owl is there, the poor wet creature!
I only hope I can quickly reach her."

She landed safely, then Brown Owl said,
"I'm soaked to the skin and I'm nearly dead!"

"I think this is fun! In better weather
Perhaps we could go for a trip together."

Now Babs balloons each Brownie day,
With Brown Owl's blessing, happy to say.

"Brown Owl, you're very quick to learn."
"To teach me ballooning is your good turn!"

52

LEND A HAND

Draw a hand by placing your own hand down flat on a piece of cardboard and drawing your pencil carefully round the outline of it.

Now you are going to live up to the Brownie motto, "Lend a Hand". In each of the fingers, on the thumb and on the palm, you can write in all the Good Turns you do in the next week. One Good Turn on each finger will give you four days, one on the thumb five, and two on the palm six and seven. Write your name on the wrist.

Fix a little support at the back by cutting a long strip of cardboard and glueing the top of it to the back of the Hand. Now carefully bend it outwards, and it will make the Hand stand up.

Your Six will find it fun to keep one of these Hands, so show yours at your next Pack meeting. If you take some pieces of card with you, the others in your Six can draw their own. Later on, your Brownie Guider may see a whole Pack of Hands!

Looking after ZOO animals

If you visit a zoo when you are studying animals for the Discoverer badge, you may think that you'd like to work in one when you grow up. With so many different animals to look after there is always plenty of work and some very unusual jobs to be done; but some of the tasks might startle you!

How would you like to give the alligators a spring-clean? During the winter months they lie sleepily on the bed of their pool and get covered in mud, foliage and queer bits and pieces, which collect in the grooves of their tough hides. When the pool has been drained, one keeper turns a hosepipe on, while another scrubs the alligator's broad back with a stiff broom.

Another hard job is polishing up the giant tortoises. First the dust must be rubbed off, then the shell wiped over with pig-oil and finally polished up till you can see your face in it. The tortoise may not think much of its spring-clean, so it's wise to keep away from its head end. The colours of the shell will come up beautifully, so Mr Tortoise may feel quite proud when the job is finished.

Perhaps you would rather groom the elephants. Every day they must be given their brush-up and shower, for they pick up a lot of dust and dirt when they roll over on the ground. Sometimes their nails may need filing, and this is done with a giant rasp and sandpaper.

The lions are very sleepy in the mornings—like some Brownies!—but most of the animals are ready for their breakfast early, especially the mountain-goats, who hardly ever seem to sleep. So are the monkeys, sea-lions and camels.

Some of the tamer lions much appreciate having their manes combed through and look very proud of themselves when their toilet is completed.

In cold weather the "chimps" welcome a nice hot cup of tea for their "elevenses". At night their keeper will sometimes hand them a few hot potatoes to use as hot-water bottles, though before morning they have often disposed of their "bottles" in a quite different way!

"This is what I call getting well oiled," says Speedy, a giant tortoise at Belle Vue Zoo, Manchester, as he gets his annual oil-and-polish

You may need a ladder when you groom a llama!

The bears must have more bread and vegetables during the winter, when they cannot depend on their large public to supply them with titbits.

Would you care to brush the teeth of the apes? This has to be done every day. Sometimes the baby monkeys have trouble cutting their teeth, so they may be given a broomstick to gnaw on.

Yes, all this is in the keeper's day's work! Do you fancy the job?

"Just where I itch!" rumbles this Whipsnade Zoo rhino, as he enjoys a wash-and-brush-up-with-manicure

A WALK IN THE COUNTRIES

by Marcia M. Armitage

Bulbuls with some Little Friends
Went for a walk one day.
Sunbeams danced around them
As they went along their way.

Bluebirds sang a pretty song
From high up in the trees,
While in and out the Primulas
Buzzed busy Little Bees.

Things are not quite as they seem,
For here's a quiz for you—
Name each Brownie and her land—
That's what you have to do.

BROWNIES Lend a Hand

by Nora Blaze

Sally had gained the House Orderly badge

"**C**ongratulations, Sally!" said the Brownie Guider. "You have gained your House Orderly badge. You worked hard for it."

Sally looked with pride at the badge with its broomhead emblem, the first one she had gained. She had enjoyed learning how to be useful in a house. Perhaps one day, when she was a grown-up, she would be married and have a house of her own to look after; she would know just how to set about keeping it clean and bright.

Miss Miller, the Assistant Brownie Guider, who was always called "Dusty", was standing near. She brought Sally out of her daydream by saying, "Would you like to put what you have learnt to good use, Sally?"

Sally looked puzzled, so Dusty went on. "My neighbour, old Miss Drew, fell down this morning and broke her arm, so she's in quite a fix. I can help her into bed tonight and dress her in the morning, and cook her breakfast, but after that I have to go to the dentist."

"Oh, poor Dusty!" sympathised Carol, another of the Kelpie Six.

"Oh, it's only a filling," Dusty answered, smiling, "but the buses don't fit in very well, so I shall be late back, and I'm worried about Miss Drew. Her sister will be arriving from Manchester tomorrow afternoon, so she will have help then, but it's the morning, you see, with the fire to make and the house to tidy and something to be got for her lunch. I won't have time to do much. Are you doing anything special in the morning, Sally?"

"Well," began Sally doubtfully, "I was going ice-skating with Carol."

"It's all right, Sally. I don't mind a bit," Carol said in her usual cheerful way. "We could go to Miss Drew's together, couldn't we? I've got the Cook badge, you know, and I can cook a meal. I always help Mum on Sundays. We can go to the ice-rink another time."

"That would be wonderful, Carol!" Dusty exclaimed, delighted. "You don't mind, do you, Sally?"

"No, of course not, Dusty," said Sally at once. "I'd like to help. What time shall we go?"

"I'm catching the half-past nine bus, so could you come about then? Do you know where I live?"

"I do," Carol said. "Your house is in the next road to ours. I've seen you go into the one on the corner."

"That's right, and Miss Drew is next to me. Hers is the bungalow with the white gate."

So at half-past nine the next morning Sally and Carol, neat and tidy in their Brownie uniforms, knocked on the door of No. 3 Grove Road. A sharp voice called "Come in!" and in they went.

Miss Drew, white-haired, one arm encased in plaster, sat bolt upright in an armchair near the sitting-room fireplace, a rug tucked round her. She stared hard at the Brownies and exclaimed, "Good gracious me! Miss Miller said she was sending two young ladies to help me."

"Miss Miller?" murmured Sally, looking puzzled.

Carol nudged her. "It's Dusty's real name, silly!"

"I didn't expect two small girls," continued Miss Drew, pursing up her mouth. "What sort of help do you imagine *you* can be?"

"We're not two small girls!" Sally protested indignantly. "We're Brownies— this is Carol and I'm Sally. And we do know how to help. I've got my House Orderly badge—look!" She pointed to it on her sleeve. "And Carol's got her

Cook badge."

Carol raised her arm and displayed her badge with the saucepan emblem.

"H'm!" Miss Drew glanced at the badges without much interest. "Well, we'll see if they mean anything. Perhaps one of you could get a fire going in here, for a start."

"I can do that." Sally smiled, although she felt more like backing out of the room and pulling Carol with her. To think they had given up their skating for this disagreeable old woman! But they had given their promise to Dusty, so they would have to stay and do their best.

"Would you mind pushing your chair back a bit, please, Miss Drew?" she asked politely.

"Whatever for, child?"

"I want to roll up the hearthrug so that I don't dirty it," Sally explained.

"Oh! Oh, very well." Miss Drew pushed back the chair, and Carol helped Sally roll up the pretty green rug.

Carol and Sally rolled up the rug

She cleaned out the grate

"Have you an old newspaper, please?"

"There's one behind you on the table," said Miss Drew shortly.

"Thank you," said Sally, taking it and spreading it out over the hearth and the carpet in front.

There were some interesting pictures that she longed to look at properly, but she dared not, feeling the old lady's disapproving gaze on her. She rolled up her sleeves and began to clean out the grate carefully so that the dust wouldn't fly all over the room. Then she drew out the ashpan, took it outside to the dust-

She emptied the ashes into the dustbin

bin, emptied it, replaced it, and began to lay the fire. Bunching up some pages of the newspaper, she pushed them into the grate, then took the other pages one by one and began rolling them up diagonally from the corner.

The old lady bent forward. "What *are* you doing, child?"

"It's to save sticks," Sally told her, wishing Miss Drew would not keep calling her "child". She might at least be nice when they had come to help her. "You roll the pages tightly like this

"It's to save sticks," explained Sally

and then twist them into a knot, and lay them with just one or two sticks and some small pieces of coal on the top."

"Oh, well, you seem to have the right idea," Miss Drew said grudgingly. "You'll find the sticks in a box under the kitchen sink."

Sally went to get them and found Carol washing up the breakfast dishes.

"Isn't she horrid!" she whispered in Carol's ear. "I wish we hadn't promised to come!"

"So do I," Carol whispered back. "We can't back out, though. I told Dusty I'd cook the lunch."

Sally filled the coal-scuttle from the shed outside and soon the fire was burning nicely. When the room was tidied and dusted, she said, "Shall we make your bed now, Miss Drew?"

"My sister can make it when she gets here," Miss Drew said in a forbidding voice. "I like my bed made properly, thank you."

"But I learnt how to make a bed properly for my badge." Sally was hurt.

"Oh, your badge! Right! Show me how to make a bed as it should be made!" Miss Drew pointed to the next room. "In there!"

The two girls opened the door and advanced on the rumpled bed. Miss Drew stood in the doorway, a look of disapproval on her face.

"You stand that side, Carol, and I'll do this side." Sally lifted off the eiderdown and bedspread and laid them carefully over a chair. "Now pull all the things back over the bed end. That's right! I'll put the pillow on the chair while we turn the mattress. Over to you! Now draw up the underblanket and sheet. Pull them up tightly, Carol, so that there aren't any creases, and tuck your side under, like this. Now I'll plump up the pillow while you fold Miss Drew's nightie. Isn't it pretty?" Sally loved pretty clothes, and Miss Drew's pink nightie had lace and little frills and tucks in it. Carol folded it neatly and placed it under the pillow.

They seized the top sheet and blankets and pulled them up to the top of the bed, turned over the tops neatly, tucked in the sides, and replaced the eiderdown and bedspread.

All this time, Miss Drew stood watching them without saying a word, but now she actually smiled.

"Yes, you *do* know how a bed should be made," she admitted. "They seem to have taught you something useful at those Brownies, after all."

"We learn how to do lots of things like that," Carol told her eagerly. "I've learnt how to cook. I can start cooking your lunch if you'll tell me what you would like."

"I should like a cup of coffee first," the old lady answered, "and I daresay you would, too."

"Oh, yes, please!" they chorused.

They were just leaving the bedroom to go into the kitchen when there was an exclamation from Miss Drew.

"My ring! I left it on the dressing-table last night. It's gone!"

"Perhaps it's fallen on the floor," Sally suggested.

She and Carol got down and crawled about the floor, peering under the dressing-table and the chest of drawers and the bed and all over the carpet.

"It isn't here, Miss Drew," said Sally at last, getting up red-faced from her efforts. "Are you sure you left it here?"

They searched the bedroom

61

"You don't mean you think Dusty — Miss Miller — took it?" Sally burst out hotly

"Of course I'm sure," snapped Miss Drew. "I always take it off before I go to bed, and put it there. You probably knocked it off, flapping the things about. Have another look! It's a diamond ring, very valuable."

They crawled all over the carpet again, but there was no sign of the ring.

"It truly isn't here, Miss Drew," Carol told her. "You must have put it somewhere else."

"No, I did not. Oh, but wait!" said Miss Drew suddenly. "Miss Miller helped me into bed last night. I must have handed it to her. What has she done with it?"

"Dusty wouldn't do *anything* with it," Carol said indignantly. "If you asked her to put it on the dressing-table that's what she would have done."

"Well, she didn't, did she?" Miss Drew sounded quite nasty. "So where is it?"

"You don't mean you think Dusty — Miss Miller — took it?" Sally burst out

hotly. "She would never do a thing like that."

Words failed them both and they stared angrily at Miss Drew, who stared angrily back.

"Of course I don't imagine that Miss Miller — Dusty, you call her? — took it. Don't be so silly. I am merely asking where she put it. I intend to ask her when she comes back! In the meantime, I'll have that coffee, if you don't mind."

They did mind. They got it ready and drank it in silence, both feeling very put out. How could Miss Drew speak like that when Dusty had been so kind! They wished more than ever that they had gone to the ice-rink.

"Well," said Miss Drew, putting down her cup, "perhaps you would now begin cooking my lunch — but not with all your hair hanging down, if you please. It's most unhygienic."

Both girls put their hands in their pockets, pulled out ribbons and tied back their long hair into neat ponytails, Carol's fair and Sally's dark. They felt better when they saw Miss Drew's surprised expression. They always kept the ribbons handy for games at Pack meetings, when their hair would be in the way.

Carol had brought an apron as well. She unrolled it and tied it round her waist.

Miss Drew went to the refrigerator and brought out two lamb chops. "Do you know how to grill these?"

"Yes, Miss Drew. And would you like me to make a pudding?"

"What kind did you have in mind?"

Carol thought. "I can make a milk pudding, if you like," she suggested, but Miss Drew shuddered and said, "No, thank you!"

Carol was quite taken aback. She adored milk puddings! Then she saw some cooking-apples on the table.

"I could stew some of those, perhaps."

"Very well. I can have them with cream."

"Shall I do the vegetables?" Sally asked.

"If you please. There are potatoes and brussels sprouts in the vegetable rack there."

The girls were working busily when there was a rattle of bottles outside. A voice shouted, "Milk-o!"

Carol opened the door to the milkman.

"Morning, Miss Drew! Hello, girls! Forty pence, please!"

"Oh, yes, it's Saturday, isn't it? Just pass my handbag, will you, Carol? It's on the dresser."

Carol handed it over and the old lady fumbled with her free hand to undo the clasp.

"I'm afraid I can't manage it. Take my purse out, will you, and pay the milkman."

Carol did so, and was closing the purse when she said "Oh!" in a startled voice.

"What's the matter?" Sally asked, looking round from the sink. The milkman had gone whistling on his way.

For answer, Carol put her fingers into the purse, drew out a glittering object, and held it up without speaking.

"My ring!" exclaimed Miss Drew. "How on earth did it get in my purse?" She stopped and went quite pink. "Oh, dear! I've just remembered. I took it off at the hospital before they put my arm in plaster. How could I have forgotten?"

"Dusty didn't have it at all!" Carol said, looking straight at her. "It was in your purse all the time."

"Oh, dear!" Miss Drew said again, leaning back heavily in her chair and looking shaken. "How dreadful of me! I am very sorry, Carol and Sally. I suppose it was all the upset yesterday that made me forget. And Miss Miller was so good, too."

"My ring!" cried Miss Drew

"Dusty *is* good," Carol answered. "We knew she wouldn't lose your ring, didn't we, Sally?"

"Of course she wouldn't!" Sally said.

Just then Dusty walked in. She was surprised at the warm welcome she received!

"How are your helpers getting along?" she asked Miss Drew.

"Splendidly, Miss Miller," the old lady replied, "really splendidly. I had no idea they could be so good. They are so young, too!"

"Ah!" said Dusty. "I sent you two of our best Brownies! I knew they would be good!"

Sally and Carol looked at each other and blushed with pride. It had all been worthwhile, just to hear Dusty say that!

Miss Drew reached for her purse and said, "I must repay them for their kindness."

"Oh, *no!*" they both cried. "We don't want paying."

"They're quite right." Dusty nodded as the old lady looked astonished. "It is one of the rules in Brownies, you see. We do good turns, but not for money."

"Oh!" said Miss Drew. "I see. Well, then, all I can do is thank you very much. And I really am sorry about the ring."

Dusty looked puzzled, but the Brownies put their hats on quickly and said goodbye.

"Phew!" said Sally as they hurried away. "What a morning!"

Carol laughed. "It was fun, though."

But that wasn't the end of it. At the next Pack meeting Dusty drew them to one side and handed them an envelope. Sally opened it wonderingly and took out two tickets.

"Miss Drew insisted that you should have them," Dusty said. "She made her sister get them specially for you. 'To make amends', she said. I suppose you know what she means. I don't!"

"Oh, Dusty!" they breathed together. "They're for the pantomime!"

"I know. I'm going with you! Do you know what the pantomime is this year?"

They both capered about gleefully, dancing round and waving the tickets.

"It's super!" cried Sally.

"It's absolutely fab!" laughed Carol. "It's 'Cinderella on Ice'!"

Play acting

These terrifying cut-throats belong to the Bosmere and Bramford District Packs

Colour slides by Rev. R. W. Francis

Sproughton (Suffolk) Brownies present a play to an appreciative audience

Above:
Georgy Porgy with one of the girls he kissed and made cry at the 10th Swindon (St. Augustine's) Pack's Revels

Colour print by Mrs Jenkins

Left:
Pirates of all shapes, sizes and colours are to be found in Swindon. These belong to the 10th Swindon (St. Augustine's) Pack

65

Where are all the Animal Lovers?

by Marcia M. Armitage

Many Brownies have pets at home, but not all of them wear the Animal Lover badge on their sleeve. Why should this be? Surely you are not leaving the care of your pet to poor Mum! This often happens, but you really miss much enjoyment if you have a pet and forget all about it.

We have some guinea-pigs. We started off with one, then decided it would be lonely and bought a mate for it. Now we have quite a colony. One of the males

is called Snuffy, and he is a comedian. He is the biggest. If his mate tries to get a piece of cabbage or a nibble at a carrot she gets pushed out of the way and even walked on. When there is the faintest sound of human life Snuffy stands at the front of his cage and chirps. Even a light switched on in the kitchen is a signal for Snuffy to sing for his supper.

If you are thinking of having a guinea-pig pet you will need a hutch for it. This should be partially separated so that one side is dark and sheltered for sleeping quarters. The other side should have fine-mesh wire across the front. The mesh must be fine because rats will attack guinea-pigs if given the chance. The hutch can be lined with straw or wood-shavings.

For diet, guinea-pigs eat greens, carrots, swedes, potatoes and cereals. In summer a pile of grass cuttings will keep a guinea-pig happy for hours. It should also have a water-pot. Guinea-pigs are rather dirty creatures and need cleaning out regularly. Do give the feeding-bowl and water-pot a good regular scrub.

If you have a pair of guinea-pigs and they have babies you should keep the babies with their mother for six weeks. We have had four litters, and it is fascinating to see how aware and lively the young ones are from the very first day. A pet shop will usually buy the babies from you, but it is wise to check on this before you put a male and female in together.

If possible, the guinea-pigs should have a pen in the garden so that they can run about in the fresh air. We have four planks which fit together with hinges so that when the animals go back in the hutch the pen can easily be put away.

Having looked after a pet of your own for three months you will be well on the way to gaining the Animal Lover badge. During this time you will have learnt about the habits, diet and care of a guinea-pig.

If you are really fond of animals and other pets you will always be on the lookout to do good turns for them. One Brownie I know takes her grandmother's dog for a walk every day. This is not only a good turn for Granny—it's a good turn for the dog too! Another Brownie who hasn't got a pet of her own collects grass and leaves for a friend's rabbit, while another one loves to groom a neighbour's dog each day and also keeps a friendly eye on the cat!

Even if you don't have a pet of your own you can do a service for the wild birds that come into your garden by making a bird-table safe from cats and keeping it supplied with titbits.

If you like animals enough to work for the Animal Lover badge you will be sure to find a way of helping towards their welfare.

The third part of the badge itself requires you to find out where and how you can get help for sick animals. If you look in the yellow pages of your local telephone directory you will find the names, addresses and telephone numbers of veterinary surgeons, the RSPCA and other organisations like the People's Dispensary for Sick Animals.

Finally, you must tell the tester the reasons why you would choose that kind of pet to own.

I am sure you will soon be wearing the Animal Lover badge on your sleeve.

ON THE NATURE TRAIL

You can have Fun Out of Doors by following this Nature trail and learning about some of the trees, shrubs, wildflowers, birds, animals and insects that make a country ramble so interesting and enjoyable. You can learn too about some of the creatures that inhabit ponds and pools. See how many creatures, trees, etc. you can name in the picture before looking up the answers.

Pipe-Cleaner Figures

David Harwood Shows You in Pictures
How to Make People and Animals with Pipe-Cleaners

If possible, use pipe-cleaners of different colours. They cost a little more than ordinary ones, but they will make your figures look much more attractive.

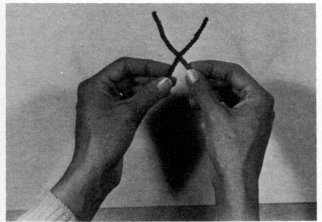

1. Take one pipe-cleaner in each hand . . .

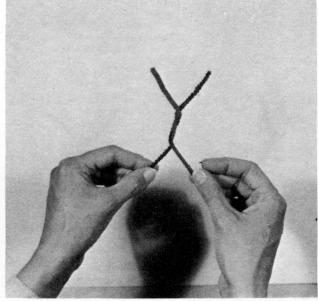

2. Twist them round each other . . .

3. Join them at the top to form the head . . .

4. Make a loop at the bottom of each for the feet . . .

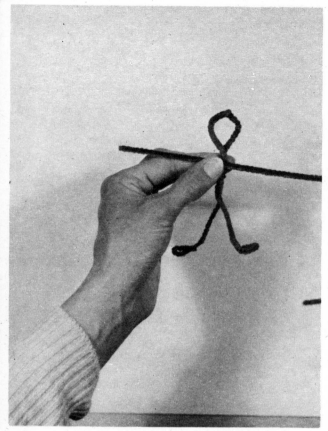

5. To make the arms, use a third cleaner and make one turn round the body section . . .

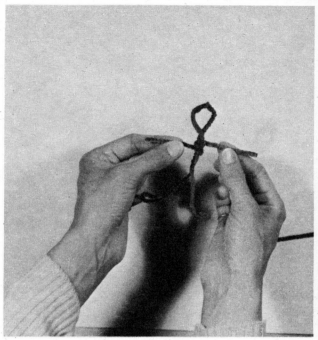

6. Make a loop at each end for the hands . . .

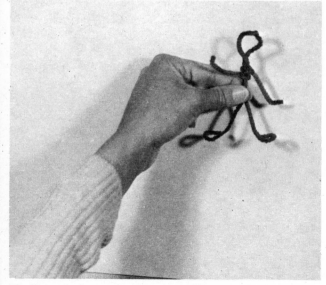

7. Bend the arms at the elbows, and you have made your first figure.

8. Now try your hand at making animals and other creatures.

On Pack holiday the Brownie Guider found an old map showing where pirate gold was hidden. The Brownies are searching for it. The only way to find it is to follow the compass directions exactly. There are deep pools, huge boulders, and treacherous quicksands on the island, so it is dangerous to stray off the right track. Can *you* find the way to the hidden treasure? Besides the compass directions, there is a clue in the verse under the old map, which runs like this:—

It isn't on the sea,
It isn't by the quay,
It isn't in the caves,
Or deep beneath the waves.

It isn't on the beach,
Or hid in Pirates' Reach.
It could be on the land
Or buried in the sand.

Where is it?

From Guider's left foot: 4E, 7N, 6E, 7S, 3E, 1N, 5E, 2N, 2W, 4N, 1E, 6S, 6E, 4N, 1E, 6S, 3N, 3W, 4N, 8W, 2N

Fun on Pack Holiday

by Rosalie Brown

The story of *Alice Through the Looking-Glass* came to life when Brownies of an Extension Pack in Perth, Scotland, went to the Brownie House at Netherurd for their annual Pack holiday. An Extension Pack consists of handicapped Brownies. With them went Extension Brownies from Glasgow and eight others who were not Extensions.

We travelled by coach and drove over the wonderful Forth Road Bridge. On arrival at the Brownie House, the cook (Red Queen) and her assistant (Red King) made tea for us and lemonade for the Brownies. Then off went the Brownies to see the bedroom.

"Double bunks—goodie! Can I sleep in the top one?"

"Not me, Brown Owl—I might fall out!"

Very soon all knew where they were to sleep and put their belongings beside their beds. Before unpacking, though, they had to see the other rooms. In the Banqueting Hall (dining-room) mugs and bowls with owls, toadstools and Brownie emblems on them were admired, and each Brownie searched for a mug with her emblem on it. The Brook (bathroom), the Queen's Parlour, and the Counting House were inspected, and only then did everyone go back Through the Looking-Glass into the bedroom again to unpack. Soon everything was neatly packed in lockers, with cases out of sight. Then it was teatime.

After tea our holiday names were given out. What laughs we had when we heard them! Jabberwocky, White Rabbit, Queen Alice, Tweedledum and Tweedledee, and so on! Our three Pack Leaders were the Rocking House Fly, Snapdragon Fly and Bread-and-Butter Fly. Then each Brownie was given a check apron in her group colour—red, blue, green or yellow—to put on for work.

From then on the holiday went with a swing. Work became play, and we had all the time in the world to do it. The White Knight on her charger (a wheelchair) held the sweeping broom while Tweedledum pushed her around. The Carpenter, who could only walk a little, was good at crawling, so there was no dust under the beds! The Red Knight, who could not grip very well, peeled some potatoes, and Hatta found her wheel-chair very handy when bringing back firewood. So everyone found she was able to do household chores and enjoy them.

Of course, it wasn't all work. We explored and collected leaves and flowers to press to make pictures for mothers. We paddled in the burn— wheel-chairs and all!—painted small dishes and hankies in the evening, and blew soap bubbles, seeing who could blow the biggest one.

One day the Black King from nowhere captured Queen Alice, the White Knight, Carpenter, Mome Rath, the King's Messenger and the White Queen and carried them away to his castle—at least, that's what he planned to do, but he became so tired that he left them in a hideout in the woods. Here the rest of the Looking-Glass people found them by following a trail of coloured thread Queen Alice had been able to drop. The Black Knight's treasure was discovered near by, and all enjoyed the lollypops.

The Wonderland Sports Day was unique; no Olympic Games were ever like these!

The last afternoon and evening were hilarious. Who were these strange, unknown, overgrown Brownies wearing up-to-date mini hemlines, and who were the creators of these fabulous hats made from leaves, pot-lids, cartons, dish-cloths, etc., all the latest Netherurd models?

So a wonderful week came to an end. In the minibus going home, we made plans to meet again the following year.

"It was lovely, Brown Owl. I want to see my mum, but I'd like to go right back again," sniffed one Brownie.

We entertained the driver of the minibus with all the songs and graces learnt during the week. He enjoyed them so much that he remarked when he dropped us off, "I'll see that my wee lassie becomes a Brownie when she reaches the right age! She's only one year old now!"

The Lady Thomson Memorial Pack Holiday House, Netherurd

On Pack Holiday

Brownies of the 3rd Clevedon West Pack on Pack holiday at Lee Bay, North Devon—
1 Enjoy a sunshine picnic
2 Prepare for battle
3 Pause for elevenses

Colour slides by Miss D. Hammond

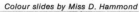

4 Brownies of the 1st Terling and 1st Great Waltham Packs, Essex, on Pack holiday at Harwich, put on life-jackets for an exciting trip by motor-launch to a lightship on the Sunk Sands

Colour slide by Mrs E. Bass

5 Well, even on Pack holiday you've got to wash. The 1st Whitstable Pack grin and bear it

Colour slide by Miss B. Rivers

6

The 13th Margate (St. Stephen's Methodist) Pack on Pack holiday at Ide Hill, near Sevenoaks—

6 Have fun in a hollow tree
7 Play in the woods
8 The "Yellow Six" wash up
9 The "Red Six" do chores out of doors

Colour slides by Miss P. Haswell

7

8

9

10 Brownies of the 1st Billingham (Teesside) Pack lay the table for an appetising meal

Colour slide by Mrs J. Heslop

10

WINTER WILD-FLOWERS

by June A. Mercer

Sometimes, during the summer months, Brownies go on wild-flower rambles, when hundreds of these can be found in bloom all over the countryside, but have you ever thought how much more exciting it would be to go on a wildflower ramble in the middle of winter? January and February seem a strange time of the year to look for wildflowers, but that is when the first of the spring blossoms begin to appear.

If you search carefully you are sure to find the **WINTER ACONITE,** which is one of the very earliest of the year's flowers. It is a pretty little flower belonging to the Buttercup family. It has clear yellow blossoms, which rest on glossy green Toby frills. The most likely place to find the Winter Aconite is under the trees, as it grows best in the shade.

A favourite with most of us is the **SNOWDROP,** which can be found soon after the Winter Aconite. We usually think of the Snowdrop as a garden flower, but it escapes from the gardens and spreads into the hedgerows and shady woods. The tiny nodding white flowers, with their six petals in two rings of three, are always a sign that spring is on the way.

The most common wildflowers to be found in January are quite often called weeds. Two of these are Groundsel and Shepherd's Purse, which are hardy plants and flower the whole year through.

GROUNDSEL belongs to the Daisy family and is one of the most common weeds in our gardens. It has a very straight stem, which can be from 6 ins. to 12 ins. high, topped with small yellow heads, and the leaves are irregular in shape. Groundsel spreads quickly over the countryside with its self-sown seeds.

SHEPHERD'S PURSE should be

quite easy for you to recognize, and it will grow in practically any soil, anywhere. It has a cluster of feather-shaped leaves growing close to the soil, from the centre of which comes a stalk of tiny white flowers. Other leaves, which grow high on the stem, are arrow-shaped with toothed edges. Shepherd's Purse gets its name because of its seed-pods. These split open to show seeds which look like coins in an old-fashioned purse.

If January is a mild month, you may get the first glimpse of the **COLTSFOOT**. This is another member of the Daisy family and recognized as one of the earliest signs of spring. At our first look at the Coltsfoot we find stout stalks topped with brilliant yellow dandelion-like flowers, but no trace of any leaves. It is easy to know the Coltsfoot once the leaves have grown. They are broad, heart-shaped, cobwebby leaves, sometimes nearly twelve inches across, and underneath the leaf it is covered with white down. The bright flower soon changes into a ball of soft white downy seeds (like a dandelion clock) and is carried away by the wind and spread far across the fields.

The next flower in our search is the **LESSER CELANDINE.** This usually appears a little later than the Coltsfoot, around the middle of February. It is a member of the Buttercup family and looks rather like a low-growing buttercup. Although it is the same golden colour as the buttercup, you would recognize it at once by its starry flowers, which may have as many as twelve petals, whereas a Buttercup only has five. If you are lucky enough to find the Lesser Celandine, pull up a plant and look at its roots. You will see that some of them are swollen into club-shaped tubers. This is where the plant stores the food which enables it to grow quickly in the early months. Look for it on sunny banks or waste ground by the roadside.

Another wildflower to be found in February is the **BARREN STRAW-BERRY.** This is a member of the Rose family and you will find it on dry banks under the shelter of a hedge. It has tiny white flowers, very similar to those of the true Wild Strawberry, to which it is closely related. It has hairy stalks and a tuft of silky leaves growing straight from the root.

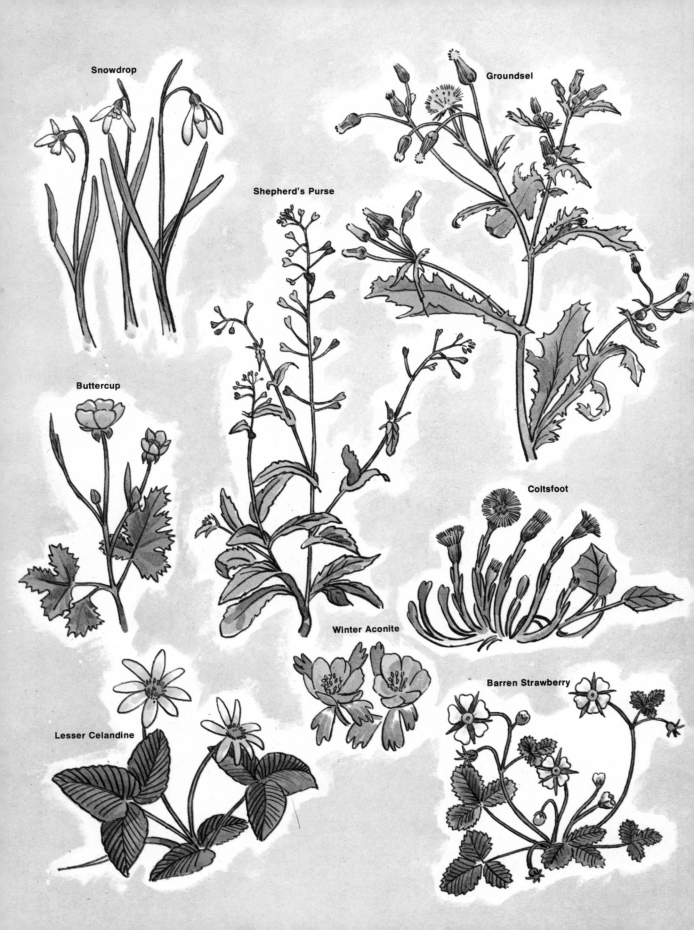

Snowdrop

Groundsel

Shepherd's Purse

Buttercup

Coltsfoot

Winter Aconite

Lesser Celandine

Barren Strawberry

WIN A BIKE AND £50 !

In this simple but exciting new competition you can win a brand-new bicycle for yourself and £50 for your Pack. Yes, this thrilling double prize could be yours!

All you have to do is to read your BROWNIE ANNUAL and then choose which you think is the best and next best story, article, puzzle, etc. of those listed in the five groups below.

The Editor has made his choice. Each BEST that agrees with his will gain five points, each NEXT BEST three points. The competitor with the highest number of points will win the grand double prize.

Group 1 Articles
A The Jeannettes of France
B Holland's Tom Thumb Town
C Looking After Zoo Animals
D Where are the Animal Lovers?
E Fun on Pack Holiday
F Winter Wildflowers

Group 2 Various
A Union Flag Game
B When the Clock Strikes Twelve
C Our Pack Holiday (verse)
D Brownie Ventures and Challenges
E Babs and Her Balloon
F Lend a Hand (verse)
G Nature Trail

Group 3 Stories
A One Day in Jordan
B A Rose for the Queen
C Barbara's Christmas Service
D The Day Everything Went Wrong
E Brownies Lend a Hand
F The Trial that Led to Adventure

Group 4 How-to-Makes
A Pretty Things
B Pipe-Cleaner Figures
C A Tree Book

Group 5 Puzzles, etc.
A Interest Badge Puzzle
B What Is It?
C Crossout Crossword
D Shop in the Supermarket
E Which Badge?
F Which Patrol?
G Cookery Signpost
H A Walk in the Countries
I Find Hidden Treasure

—F

The Brownie Annual 1975 Competition Entry Form

Just write down the letter that is set against the title of your choice in the list in the first column.

GROUP 1 ARTICLES	Best	B
	Next Best	E
GROUP 2 VARIOUS	Best	E
	Next Best	G
GROUP 3 STORIES	Best	E
	Next Best	C
GROUP 4 HOW-TO-MAKES	Best	A
	Next Best	C
GROUP 5 PUZZLES, ETC.	Best	D
	Next Best	G

My Name is Nicola Johnston

My Address is 65, Winfield Ave. Colinton Edin.

My Age is 11 yrs

My Pack is ....

My Guider's Name and Address is Sheila Armstrong

81

What I like most about the Brownie Annual

The Brownie Annual 1975 "Win a Bike and £50" Competition

Don't miss entering this new "double-prize" competition and giving yourself the chance of winning a handsome brand-new bicycle and £50 for your Pack.

The competition gives every Brownie, regardless of age, an equal chance.

First, enjoy your *Brownie Annual*, which is packed with stories, articles, puzzles and pictures specially written and chosen for Brownies. Then write down in a simple, straightforward way what you like most about the BROWNIE ANNUAL—its looks, the ideas it gives you, the information you get from it, the puzzles that keep you occupied, the pleasures you get from the stories, the pictures of Brownie activities, or anything else about it that you specially like.

Your little write-up will be taken into account if there should be competitors with equal points.

If you win and would rather have something else of equal value to the bicycle you may do so.

When you have completed both front and back of the entry form, cut it out and put it in an envelope, and post to THE BROWNIE ANNUAL 1975 COMPETITION, PURNELL BOOKS, BERKSHIRE HOUSE, QUEEN STREET, MAIDENHEAD, BERKSHIRE, SL6 1NF.

Your entry must arrive not later than March 31st, 1975. The winner will be notified and the prizes awarded as soon after this date as possible.

The publishers' decision is final, and no correspondence will be entered into in connection with the competition.

Winner of the 1974 prize competition was Sally England, of the 22nd Rugby Pack.

Lend a Hand

by Edna Gilbert

Upon the meadows snow lies deep,
And high upon the hill
The children shout and laugh and play,
As children will.

The pond is frozen, nothing stirs;
The shrubs and trees seem dead,
And from the little creatures wild
All warmth has fled.

Do you remember, last July,
A robin on the lawn,
A blackbird's song that woke you up
Each golden dawn?

Do you recall the nesting time,
A fledgling's hungry cry,
The day it flew on quivering wings
Up to the sky?

Where are they now, the singing
    birds,
As winter's cold winds blow
And all their food is buried deep
Beneath the snow?

You want to help? I knew you would!
Start this good turn today!
Collect food scraps and feed the
    birds
That come your way.

Then they'll be back. Their joyous songs
Will make the woodlands ring
If we just think and LEND A HAND
Until the spring.

The trail that led to ADVENTURE

by Murray Collier

"This time," Rosemary said, pulling her woolly hat further down on her head, "we really *are* lost!"

Jean, Second of the Pixies, paused for a moment while trying to brush some of the leaves from her Brownie uniform and gazed round the wood. The two Brownies were standing on a narrow path with trees crowding so close to it that they met overhead. It was quite gloomy, although both girls knew that the sun was shining brightly outside the wood.

"Well, at least we are on a path now," Jean said, turning her attention to some twigs caught in her long, fair plaits. "I was getting tired, pushing my way through those bushes."

"We really are lost"

Rosemary hitched up the small haversack containing the items they had collected for their Nature box. "Which way should we go?" she wondered aloud. "It's ages since we left Brown Owl, and she will be getting worried. She told us to stay in sight of the clearing."

Rosemary was Sixer of the Pixies, and Jean was her best friend. Together with the other Brownies, they were spending a day in Hainault Woods, finding specimens for the Nature boxes which each Six was making. Each Sixer had been given an area on the edge of the clearing where Mrs Drake, the Brownie Guider, had parked the minibus. Somehow, Rosemary and Jean had wandered too far from the clearing and were lost.

Jean finished tidying herself and looked up and down the path, hoping to find a clue which would show her the right direction. But the path just wandered off through the trees with no indication of where it came from or where it led to.

"Well, which way?" Rosemary asked, tucking some of her dark, unruly curls back under her hat. "It's no use just standing here."

"Oooh—look at this!" Wide-eyed, Jean pointed to a track in a patch of damp earth.

The two girls knelt to examine it. "Is it a wolf's track?" Jean asked, looking fearfully round.

Rosemary laughed scornfully. "Don't be silly—there aren't any wolves around now! It might be a fox's, though." She, too, peered rather nervously through the trees.

"Isn't it *big*?" Jean whispered, tracing the track with the tip of one finger. "It must be quite a large animal."

"Oh, this is silly," Rosemary said, standing up. "It's just a big dog, I expect. Come on!"

"We're not going *that* way, are we?" Jean asked in surprise as Rosemary walked down the path in the direction the track led.

"Well, perhaps our animal knows where it is going—*we* certainly don't!" Rosemary called back over her shoulder. "Come on!"

Jean hesitated, then, rather than be left alone, she hurried after Rosemary. At the first turn in the path they saw a gleam of sunlight and a moment later emerged thankfully into a small clearing. Both girls immediately felt better, with the gloom of the wood behind them.

"There's a wider path over there," Rosemary pointed. "Shall we——?"

She broke off as Jean gave a scream and clutched at her. With a deep *wooof* a long brown-and-white animal bounded from the bushes and raced toward them. Then it stopped, sat down and put its head on one side, a sad, puzzled expression on its face.

Jean and Rosemary stared back at it for a moment, then the Sixer burst out laughing. "It's a basset hound!" she cried. She snapped her fingers. "Here, boy!"

The dog wagged its tail uncertainly, then stood up and moved slowly forward,

"Is it a wolf's track?"

sniffing cautiously at Rosemary's outstretched fingers. Satisfied at last, it licked her hand and then rolled over on its back, waving four enormous paws in the air.

Jean laughed delightedly. "Look! You can see where our tracks came from. I've never seen such big paws on such a small dog."

"He's not so small," Rosemary said, tickling the dog's tummy. "Look how long his body is. Bassets are really much bigger than they look, but because they have such short legs people *think* they are small. Don't you remember? Aunt Rose had one. They are quite expensive dogs to buy."

"Perhaps he's lost, like us," Jean suggested. "Look, there's a tag on his collar."

Rosemary turned the little disc over. *"Belinda, The Ridings, Hainault,"* she read out. "Well, our boy dog is a girl dog."

At that moment the basset gave a squirm and sat up, looking at the two Brownies with its drooping eyes below a forehead wrinkled with worry lines. Both girls burst out laughing at the sad-looking sight it presented.

"They are such jolly dogs, really,"

Rosemary laughed, "but they always look so miserable."

"Oh, look!" Jean cried suddenly. "Look at her ear!"

Belinda's long, silky ears, hanging down the sides of her face like a judge's wig, looked as though they had just been ironed, but the bottom edge of the left ear had a wide strip of sticking-plaster along it.

"I expect she hurt it and her owner put that on," Rosemary said. "Anyway, we'd better see if we can *find* her owner —and Brown Owl, too!"

She fished in the haversack and brought out a length of string, which she slipped through Belinda's collar. "Come on, old girl," she said. "Show us which way to go."

"Listen!" Jean said, as they were about to move off. "I heard a car—over there!" She pointed down the path opposite them.

They hurried along, with the dog trotting happily at their side. The path proved to be short, leading into a much bigger clearing with a few cars parked round the edges of it.

"I know where we are," said Jean, with relief. "Brown Owl has parked the minibus at the other end of the clearing, near the road."

"Belinda!" a voice called suddenly.

The dog's head swung round, then with a deep *wooof* Belinda pulled the string loose from Rosemary's hand and sped away to a man standing by one of the cars. He bent down and made a fuss of the dog, then walked over to the two Brownies, with Belinda prancing round him.

"Oh, look!" cried Jean. "Look at her ear!"

"Did you find my lost dog?" he asked. "I was beginning to worry about her."

"*She* found *us*," Rosemary told him. "We followed her trail—we were lost—and she came back and found us."

"We thought she might be a wolf, really," Jean told him. "Her tracks were so big."

The man laughed. "It's those great paws of hers—clumsy things!"

"How did she hurt her ear?" Rosemary asked.

The man laughed again and rubbed Belinda's head affectionately. "Well, bassets are very greedy dogs and gulp their food down as fast as they can. Yesterday she was in such a hurry that she let her ear hang in her bowl—and she bit it!"

The two Brownies laughed.

"Fancy biting your own ear!" Jean chortled. "I'll bet that put her off her dinner!"

"Oh, no, it didn't," the man assured them. "She wouldn't let me touch her ear until she had cleaned up her bowl."

Rosemary and Jean petted the dog for a few moments and then said that they must be getting back. The man put his hand into his pocket, but, guessing what he was going to do, both Brownies stepped back.

"I must give you a little reward for finding Belinda," he said. "Apart from her being quite a valuable dog, I would have spent half the afternoon looking for her."

Rosemary shook her head. "That was our good turn, and, anyway, we have enjoyed meeting Belinda."

"Stormont Belinda of Avonmouth—that's her full name," Belinda's owner told them. "I think *she* should say thank you as well. Belinda," he said to the dog, "say thank you."

He made a fuss of the dog

The basset sat down and solemnly raised a large paw, which each girl shook. Then her owner knelt to remove Rosemary's piece of string.

"Hallo! Lucky that didn't happen earlier or you wouldn't have known her name," he said, showing them the disc from Belinda's collar, which had just broken off in his hand. "Now, come on, my girl! I've got a bowl of food in the car for you and some sandwiches for me. I want a quiet afternoon, and I don't want to go hunting all over the woods for lost dogs."

With another word of thanks to the Brownies, he walked off, with Belinda trotting close on his heels.

"Don't let her bite her ear!" Jean called after him.

Rosemary and Jean hurried to the far end of the clearing, and suddenly heard

Mrs Drake calling. Hurrying on, they were thankful to see their Guider. A picnic was laid out beside the minibus.

"Wherever have you two been?" Mrs Drake asked. "I've sent the others to look for you."

The two girls explained that they had wandered from the path.

"Well, I hope you've brought back some good specimens to make up for the anxiety you've caused," said Mrs Drake.

Soon the other Brownies returned, and they all had a happy picnic, later showing each other the Nature specimens they had collected. The rest of the afternoon was spent playing games in the warm sun-shine, and Rosemary and Jean recounted the story of Belinda.

At last it was time to leave and they all climbed into the minibus. They sang as Mrs Drake drove slowly down the forest lane and out on to the main road. Jean glanced back and saw that Belinda's owner's car was still at the far end of the clearing.

Traffic was quite heavy at first and Mrs Drake was forced to drive slowly. At one point they had to stop, and Rosemary saw a car at the side of the road with the bonnet up and a man working on the engine.

"Poor chap!" Mrs Drake said, sympa-

88

"Wherever have you two been?" asked the Brownie Guider

"Which of you is on the trail of a stolen dog?" asked the policeman

thetically, but Rosemary and Jean weren't listening. They were staring at the dog that was pawing at the rear window of the car, barking frantically.

"Belinda!" they both exclaimed.

"But that's not Belinda's owner—he's still back in the woods, I saw him!" Jean cried.

The traffic thinned and Mrs Drake was able to move off, increasing speed on the clearer road and leaving the parked car far behind. Jean was scribbling the car's number on the paper in which her sandwiches had been wrapped.

"Oh, Brown Owl, do stop!" Rosemary begged. "That was Belinda in that car. I'm sure she's been stolen."

"Come, now!" Mrs Drake said, keeping her eyes on the road ahead. "It was probably just another basset hound that looked like your Belinda."

"It wasn't, it wasn't, Brown Owl!" Jean

insisted desperately. "It *was* Belinda. I saw the plaster on her ear."

"That dog did have some plaster on its ear, Brown Owl," Pamela, one of the other Sixers, confirmed.

Rosemary and Jean continued to plead with Mrs Drake until at last the Guider gave a left-turn signal and pulled out of the traffic into a lay-by. "We'll see what the police think about it," she said, and the Brownies saw a police car parked in the lay-by.

"Stay there until I send for you," she told the two girls, and walked across to the police car. She chatted to the policemen for a moment, and then one of them came across to the minibus.

"Well, which of you is on the trail of a stolen dog?" he asked, smiling.

Rosemary and Jean scrambled out and told him their story. Jean thrust the sandwich paper with the car number on it

"What's the trouble, officer?"

car, which is why he's kicking up all that din. Shut up, Rover!'' Such was the power of the man's voice that the dog cowered down in the car and was silent. The man turned back in satisfaction to the policeman. "See? Does just as his master tells him."

"Perhaps you'd be good enough to step out here and show me your driving licence, sir," the policeman said. "I won't detain you long."

With every appearance of goodwill the man did so. While he was talking to the policeman Rosemary walked quietly round to the back of the car and tried the door handle. It turned, and she eased the door open slightly, slipped her hand through and pulled the string loose from the dog's collar. Leaving the door slightly ajar, she

under his nose. "It was a red car," she said, "one of those with doors at the back; not a van, though."

"An estate car?" the policeman asked, evidently impressed.

Jean suddenly grabbed his arm and pointed back down the road. "Look! I think this is it now."

The policeman glanced at the number on the paper, then at the approaching car. To the girls' relief, he stepped into the road and signalled the driver to pull in to the lay-by.

The driver poked his head out of the window. "What's the trouble, officer? Not going too fast, was I?"

"No, sir," the policeman said. "Is that your dog in the back there?" He pointed to where a basset hound with plaster on one ear was tied by a piece of string to the rear door-handle. The dog was barking furiously.

"What old – er – Rover there? Of course he's mine! He doesn't like travelling by

The dog pushed open the door and ran out

Belinda was delighted to see her master again

walked back to stand beside the police-man.

"Belinda—here, girl!" she called suddenly, and with a deep *wooof* the dog pushed open the door and raced round to the two Brownies, prancing delightedly when she reached them.

"I thought you said her name was Rover?" Mrs Drake said to the man.

"Now, look here——" the man began angrily, but Jean interrupted him by giving a shout and racing to the edge of the road, where she signalled frantically to an approaching car. It swung into the lay-by and Belinda's owner leaned out of the window.

"Hello, you two!" he said. "I've lost that dog of mine again. I'm just going to phone my wife that I'll be late——"

He, too, was interrupted, this time by a long brown-and-white streak that hurtled up to the car and began licking his face. Belinda was obviously delighted to see her master again.

After that it was soon all over. The police took a note of the two Brownies' addresses and then made the man who had stolen Belinda go with them to the police-station. Before he followed them, Belinda's owner spoke to Mrs Drake and the two girls.

"This time you must accept a reward," he said. "That was a very clever piece of work. In a little while Belinda will have some puppies. I want you to have one. Here is my card." He passed a card to Mrs Drake. "Perhaps you would be good enough to see these girls' parents and ask their permission for them to have a puppy. Let me know what they say and I'll pop over and see them."

Mrs Drake looked at the shining eyes of the two Brownies. "Well, they will have a little time to persuade their parents," she said. "Somehow I think they'll succeed!"

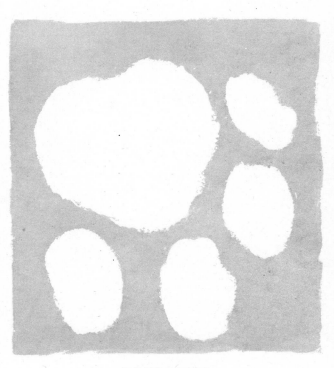

Belinda's pawprints

Make a Tree Book

Anne Phillips Shows You How

The other day I had a very interesting letter from a Brownie Guide named Norma, who lives near Melbourne, in the sunny land of Australia. She had made trips into the lovely countryside to look at trees. She noticed the shape of the different trees, made bark rubbings, and brought different kinds of leaves home with her. Then she set to work and put all her findings into what she called her "Tree Book".

I wondered if you would like to make one too. I am sure that it would help you with the Discoverer badge.

Norma used an ordinary exercise book. It would be fun to make your own, wouldn't it?

You need: two sheets of thin cardboard, each about 15cm (6 ins.) by 23cm (9 ins.), twenty sheets of drawing-paper the same size, and a piece of ribbon or cord.

Along the long side of the cardboard and drawing-paper make a little hole at 10cm (4 ins.) and another at 13cm (5 ins.). Be careful when you do this.

Now work out a design for the cover of your Tree Book. It could look something like the drawing opposite.

Now put your cardboard and your drawing-sheets together and fasten them by threading ribbon or cord through the little holes in one side and tying a bow. It is very useful to have loose sheets fastened together in this way, for if you make a mistake you can easily take one page out and put another in its place.

When your book is ready, go out into the woods and fields and see how many different kinds of trees you can find. Here are the names of some well-known one: horsechestnut, beech, oak, ash, elm, silver birch (which has silvery bark), sycamore, poplar and larch.

Draw the shape of each tree you choose and take a leaf from it. Make a bark rubbing too. How do you do this? Put a piece of fairly thick white paper or greaseproof paper against the bark of the tree, hold the paper firmly and rub up and down it with a black or brown wax crayon. When you take the paper away, you will find that you have a pattern on it which is the same as that on the tree-trunk.

Now arrange the first two pages of your book to look like the other drawing on this page. You could make a "print" of the leaf by laying it face downwards on a table, then covering it with thin paper. Scribble all over the back with a crayon, a coloured pencil or a soft black pencil. The leaf with all its tiny veins will appear. Stick the "print" and the bark rubbing on with tiny pieces of sticky tape.

Use two pages of your book for each tree and add anything else you know about it. There may be some trees that you do not know, so do try and find out what they are. Your teacher at school or your Guider would help you.

You will have as much fun making your Tree Book as Norma in Australia had in making hers.